From Glen to Glen

Roe Valley Tales Re-told

Mary Ellen Hayward

Love,

Mary Ellen

HAYBALE PUBLICATIONS

FIRST PUBLISHED IN NORTHERN IRELAND
BY HAYBALE PUBLICATIONS 2010

www.haybalepublishing.co.uk

ISBN: 978-0-9565454-0-4

PRINTED BY LIMAVADY PRINTING COMPANY
PHOTOGRAPHY: JASON BELL, DENIS HEGARTY,
BRENDAN McMENAMIN
AND LIMAVADY BOROUGH COUNCIL

ILLUSTRATIONS BY GAVIN MULLAN
MAPS BY MARK HAYWARD

Dedicated to the memory of
Paul Hayward
who loved this landscape

Contents

Acknowledgements

I want to express my gratitude to all those writers who have researched and published material on the myths and legends of the Roe Valley over the years.

I am grateful to my nephew, Gavin Mullan for the illustrations. Thanks to Felicity McCall for writing such a generous foreword and Helen Mark, Ken McCormick and John Brown for taking the time to read and comment on my manuscript.

I am indebted to Mickey Kane for reading the text at an early stage. Without his belief in the project, his enthusiasm, support and good humour, this publication would never have seen the light of day. Sincere thanks to Deirdre Devine for her friendship, encouragement, wisdom and advice. Many thanks to my editor, Anne Mullan, and to the library staff in Limavady.

I would like to acknowledge the contribution of my late son, Paul, who took an active interest in helping me with all aspects of this collection. A very special note of thanks to my husband Graham and sons Kevin and Mark for walking every step of the way with me.

I want to thank the staff and pupils from: Limavady High School, St. Mary's School in Limavady, and St. Patrick's & St. Brigid's in Claudy for their initial participation in reading the tales, and for their superb interpretations which resulted in the 'Glen to Glen' Art Exhibitions. Thanks to Limavady Borough Council for their generous prizes. For accommodating the exhibitions – my thanks to Tesco in Limavady and to the Diamond Centre in Claudy.

I am grateful to all who contributed poems and photographs. Thanks to Seamus and Anne Mullan for backing the project. I am ever grateful to the members of the Jane Ross Writing Group in Limavady, whose warmth, friendship and encouragement have sustained me.

Mary Ellen Hayward

Foreword

Nowhere is the richness of our culture and heritage more vibrantly reflected than in the myths and legends specific to one area, unique in their sense of time and place, culture and identity. They have been passed down through the generations, no doubt embellished or altered in detail, but always remaining true to the spirit of the stories whose origins are obscured in time. Mary E Hayward is a master storyteller whose love for and fascination with the legends drawn from her native Borough of Limavady have prompted her to collect them in this very special illustrated volume. They are, in her own words,'re-imagined, and brought up to date.' So let the author lead you through this collection of tales which weave together the mythical and magical, factual and faery. Enjoy, tell and re- tell, and ensure these well-loved tales survive to entertain and delight generations yet unborn.

Felicity McCaul, writer and playwright.

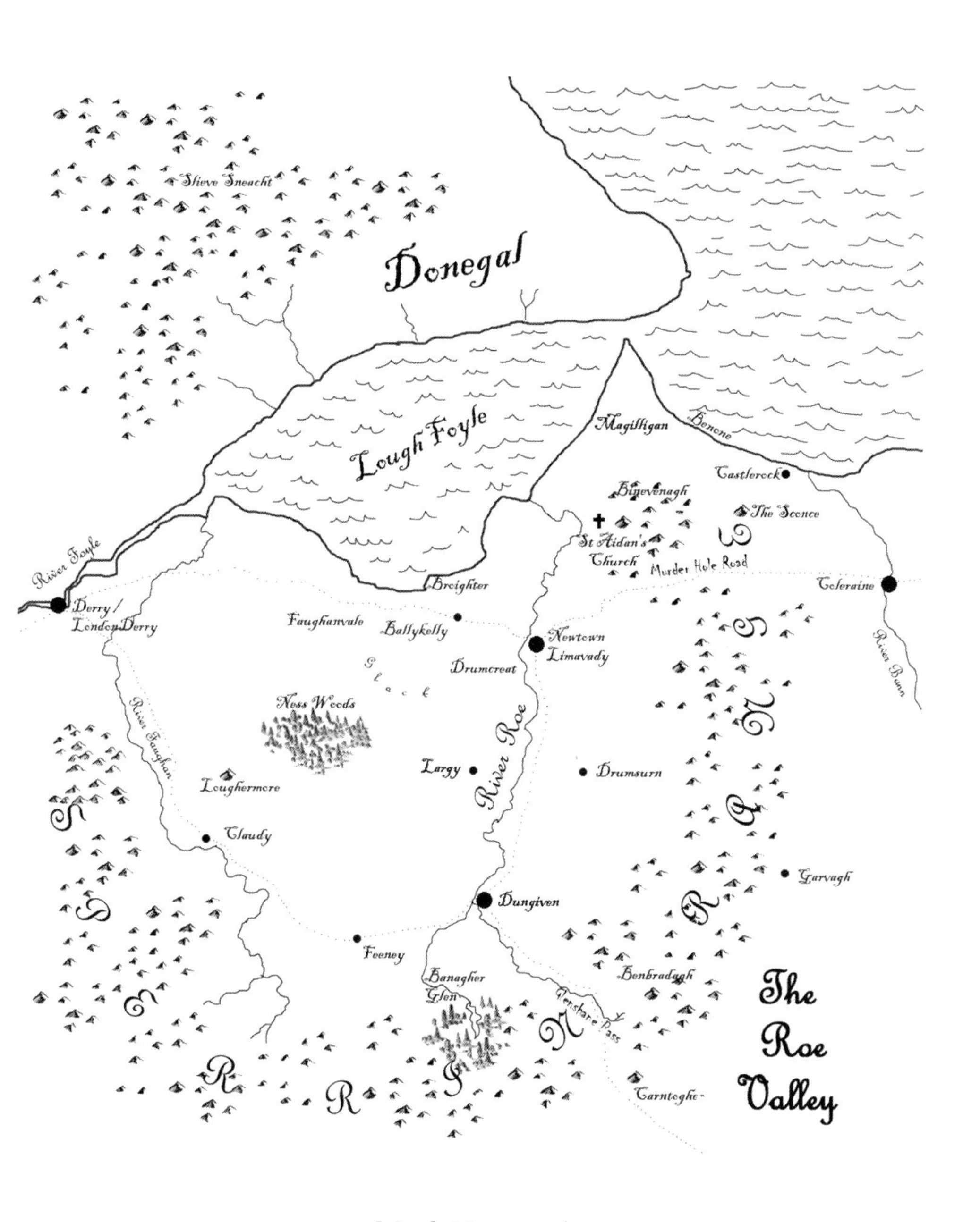

Slieve Sneacht
Donegal
Lough Foyle
River Foyle
Magilligan
Benone
Castlerock
Binevenagh
The Sconce
St Aidan's Church
Murder Hole Road
Coleraine
Breighter
Derry / LondonDerry
Faughanvale
Ballykelly
Newtown Limavady
Drumcreat
Glack
River Bann
Ness Woods
River Faughan
River Roe
Largy
Drumsurn
Loughermore
Claudy
Garvagh
Dungiven
Feeney
Banagher Glen
Benbradagh
Glenshane Pass
Carntoghe
The Roe Valley

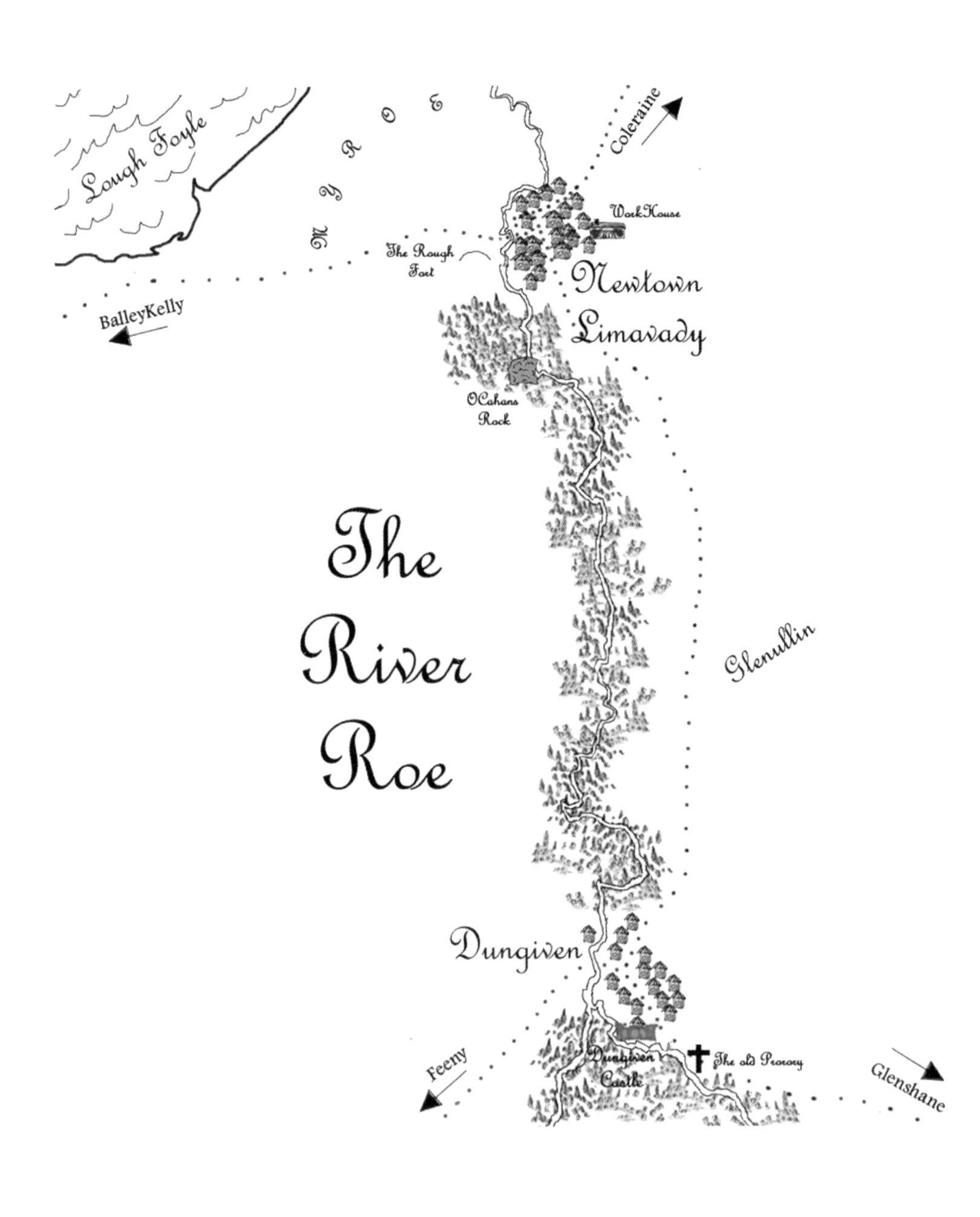

Mark Hayward

Danny Boy

Introduction

I turn left at Bovally, in Limavady, and come across a housing estate which looks as if it has been built in the past ten years, or thereabouts. The street names intrigue me: McCurry Walk, Rory Dall Drive, Petrie Place, Rossair, Hempsonvale, Weatherly Way, Danny Boy Place. This starts me wondering about the past. Where do those names come from?

I know there is a link with Danny Boy - the Londonderry Air, as it is also called. I drive home, full of curiosity, to begin my research.

Danny Boy
Part One

Rory Dall O'Cahan

(Some time between 1500 and 1650)

Rory O'Cahan was a bonny baby with a shock of dark curly hair, bright blue eyes and a wail that could wake the dead. A sturdy child, he loved to roll around the floor in mock battle with his siblings. When he was bored eating the soft milky food of the nursery he would often sneak into the kitchen, looking for cakes and sweetmeats. He was one of the famous O'Cahans who, at one time, ruled the whole of the Roe Valley and most of the land between the River Bann and the Foyle.

When Rory was just four years old he became ill with smallpox. Nobody expected him to live but, against the odds, he recovered. Unfortunately the illness robbed him of his eyesight, after which he became known as Rory Dall (Blind Rory).

Rory grew up without learning the skills of reading, archery, hunting and soldiering - the usual pastimes of O'Cahan men. He could however, tell people apart, from the scent of their clothes or the speed of their walk – before they even opened their mouths in greeting. Rory Dall was determined not to waste his life feeling sorry for himself.

In those far off days there was not much opportunity for a blind man to earn his own living but Rory Dall had a gift for music and learned to play the harp, as soon as he was tall enough to reach the strings. He loved traditional tunes that had been passed down through the generations and enjoyed composing his own. He had an amazing memory: after hearing a tune once he could reproduce it perfectly.

Rory's talent and large repertoire enabled him to travel the length and breadth of Ireland and Scotland, playing in the grand houses of noblemen and chieftains. He composed famous tunes: Ae Fond Kiss and Tabhair Dom do Lámh (Give me your Hand) – both of which appeared in Irish music charts in the 1970s. Robbie Burns, the famous Scottish poet, wrote lyrics for Ae Fond Kiss.

One midsummer's eve the O'Cahans threw a big party at their castle on the banks of the Roe. The air reverberated with music and laughter. They brewed beer and distilled whiskey. Tables groaned under the weight of food: venison, pigeon, salmon, beef, pork, cabbage, beetroot, mushrooms, onions, garlic - all flavoured with honeyed sauces and garnished with wild sorrel.

When the party began Rory Dall was in good spirits; he loved music and banter. The conversation soon turned to the English who had conquered most of Ireland. Some chieftains had given their lands to Queen Elizabeth, in exchange for money and honours, before changing sides and joining rebellions against her. It seemed to Rory Dall that it would be only a matter of time before the English, with their superior armies and vast amounts of wealth, would take over land which O'Cahans had ruled for centuries. As he sat in the corner, knocking back whiskey, his head began to swirl unpleasantly; he felt unwell.

Outside, in the balmy summer air, Rory felt better. He staggered down by the ford in the River Roe before collapsing on a soft ferny bed. Lying there, blissfully asleep, he heard faeries playing a beautiful, haunting tune.

Rory Dall awoke; his tongue felt as sour as buttermilk and as thick as a giant mushroom. He sat by the river, not hearing foxes' barks or rustlings in the undergrowth. The magical music consumed his thoughts: he was unsure whether it had all been a dream, fuelled by too much drink, or whether it was a real faery tune. The melody stayed in Rory Dall's head as he walked home. It seemed to reflect the O'Cahans' sense of impending doom: O'Cahan's Lament would be an apt name for it.

Meanwhile the party was in full swing. The smell of hounds picking on bones and leftovers lingered in the air as Rory returned to the castle. He picked up his harp and, as he plucked the first notes of his new tune, O'Cahan's Lament, a hush fell upon the crowd. Many guests felt so moved by the music that tears flowed down their cheeks.

Rory Dall rarely played O'Cahan's lament. Although at first he wanted to make it famous, he was afraid that the faeries, not liking him stealing their tune, would inflict even more destruction on the O'Cahan clan. The air, however, stayed in the hearts and minds of everyone who heard it, both at home in Ulster and in the courts of Scotland. Eventually it became known, all over the world, as The Londonderry Air, and later as Danny Boy.

Note

Rory Dall O'Cahan died and was buried on the Isle of Skye. His harp and tuning key were treasured and kept there, in one of the great houses, for many years. When another O'Cahan musician travelled to Skye, the harp was given to him to bring home to Rory Dall's beloved Roe Valley.

Danny Boy /The Londonderry Air

Oh Danny boy, the pipes, the pipes are calling
From glen to glen, and down the mountain side.
The summer's gone, and all the flowers are dying.
'Tis you, 'tis you must go and I must bide.

But come ye back when summer's in the meadow
Or when the valley's hushed and white with snow.
'Tis I'll be here in sunshine or in shadow
Oh Danny boy, oh Danny boy, I love you so.

And if you come, when all the flowers are dying
And I am dead, as dead I well may be
You'll come and find the place where I am lying
And kneel and say an "Ave" there for me.

And I shall hear, tho' soft you tread above me
And all my dreams will warm and sweeter be
If you'll not fail to tell me that you love me
I'll simply sleep in peace until you come to me.

I'll simply sleep in peace until you come to me.

(Words by Fred Weatherly)

A copy of the famous Downhill Harp.

Danny Boy
Chapter Two

Denis O'Hempsey

(Blind Harper 1695-1807)

Mrs O'Hempsey was smiling as she stood in her doorway, leaning against the jamb. Denis, her four-year-old son, was rattling out rhythms on the ground, and on the walls of the house, with his walking stick. She was delighted by his progress: a year ago she had feared for his life when he became ill.

At first they thought Denis had a chill, winter was unusually cold and damp, but they knew it was the dreaded smallpox when pus-filled blisters appeared on his limbs and face. With the help of many lotions, potions and prayers Denis made a good recovery. Eye-infections lasted too long however, and he lost his eyesight.

Denis could not see, so he listened attentively. He could hear rhythms in everything: people's speech, the way they walked and breathed, the sounds of waves, wind and rain battering on the thatch and stone walls of his house in Craigmore, near Garvagh. He would hum and make music with his fingers, feet, tongue, voice – anything that made noise.

Denis' siblings considered him a sop, a mammy's boy. In springtime, while they were busy cutting or spreading turf, fishing, snaring rabbits or churning butter, he would be dreaming of faraway places. He loved potatoes mashed with scallions and, when no-one was around, skimmed cream from the top of the milk with cupped hands that were far from clean. He licked every last drop of cream from his fingers, safe in the knowledge that he would not feel the sting of the sally rod across the back of his legs – a fate that regularly befell his brothers and sisters for the same misdemeanour.

In his final years Denis boasted that his long and healthy life – he lived to be one hundred and twelve – was the result of a diet of milk, champ and water: nothing else had ever entered his mouth.

When Denis was twelve years old he went to work for George Canning in Garvagh. It was there that his musical education began. His teacher, Brigid O'Cahan, was astonished at his gift. She taught him all the tunes that had been handed down to her from Rory Dall O'Cahan, her ancestor. The tune he loved the most was O'Cahan's Lament, renamed Aislinn Ógfear (The Young Man's Dream), now known as Danny Boy or The Londonderry Air. He excelled at The Minstrel's Farewell, Ae Fond Kiss and Tabhair Dom do Lámbh (Give Me Your Hand), giving them a sad plaintive air. These tunes are still played today.

To help Denis embark on his professional career as a musician, the people of Garvagh organised a collection and asked Conor O'Kelly, from Draperstown, to design and produce a harp for him. The harp which Conor constructed was no ordinary harp: made of willow and fir, its back was carved from a single piece of fir which was thousands of years old and dug out of a bog above Downhill. Conor strung it with the best brass wire he could find. Denis treasured that harp throughout his lifetime; it eventually became known as the Downhill Harp.

With his new instrument, eighteen-year-old Denis began working as a travelling musician: he boasted of having played in every single townland in Ireland and Scotland. He was away from home for more than a decade at a time and returned to each place with a wealth of tunes and stories which captivated audiences. In every nobleman's house Denis was highly regarded for his wonderful musicianship and storytelling skills. Whenever there was interesting gossip in a big house which Denis was visiting, he turned it into a story to tell at the next house. Denis memorised all of his stories and tunes.

In 1745 Denis was aged fifty and, while on a second tour of Scotland, he was asked to go to Edinburgh to play for Bonnie Prince Charlie.

Denis felt privileged as he entered the great hall, feeling his way with a cane. Soon his senses were overwhelmed by smells and sounds: pots and pans rattled in the kitchen; cooking smells of capons, cabbage, eels, goose-fat, and the sweet tang of cider, hung in the air. Denis wondered how wealthy people could stomach so much food: they ate for hours, to the skirl of bagpipes.

At last they moved from long tables to great comfortable chairs which had been stuffed with horsehair and covered in tapestries that mirrored heathers and angry winter skies. Denis took a seat and placed the harp next to his heart. A sudden hush fell upon the crowd. [Nowadays harpists place the harp on the right side of the chest.] As the sweet notes of Aislinn Ógfear (Danny Boy) filled the air, Bonnie Prince Charlie was moved to tears – he was far from his home in Rome and the music touched his soul.

To cheer the prince, four fiddlers joined Denis; they played "The King Shall Come Into His Own", a popular Scottish jig. Soon the young prince was up dancing, tears forgotten.

When he was aged eighty-six Denis met, and married, a Magilligan woman. He joked that the devil himself must have brought them together: he was old and blind, had a hump on his back and a single row of rotten teeth – all she had wrong with her was a bit of a limp! They lived in a cottage in Ballymacarry, near Magilligan. In his eighty-seventh year Denis became the proud father of a baby girl, making him the envy of every old bachelor in the parish.

In 1791 the government became worried that, with the deaths of the great bards and old-style musicians and poets, ancient Irish tunes and poems would vanish into the mists of time. Edward Bunting, an eighteen-year-old musician, was given the job of collecting, and writing down, ancient Irish harp music.

Ten of the best harpers in the country were invited to a Great Harp Festival in Belfast and, aged ninety-seven, Denis O'Hempsey was the oldest musician present. He played his harp in the traditional manner, placing the instrument next to his heart and, using his long gnarled nails, strummed the chords and picked out the notes.

Three prizes were awarded; much to Denis' surprise, he was not among the winners. Maybe he was not as sharp as he had been in earlier years, or maybe he had boasted too much about how good he was. Nonetheless, he received six guineas for his participation.

Soon afterwards Edward Bunting arrived at O'Hempsey's house, to write down the musical notes of all his tunes, including Aislinn Ógfear. Bunting, who was not a harper, arranged the music for piano, and made a number of mistakes, but his manuscripts were destined to be passed on to future generations.

Denis was a hundred and twelve, and dying, when, one day, his daughter told him that Rev Sir Harvey Bruce was coming to visit. Not wanting the reverend gentleman to know he was at death's door, Denis asked his daughter to prop him up in bed, holding a harp.

The visitor entered. Denis played a few chords on his beloved harp, collapsed on the bed and gave up his spirit.

Note

Denis O'Hempsey's legacy lives on in a treasure-trove of tunes that are every bit as well known and loved today as they were two centuries ago. He is recognised as the last of the true bards of Ireland.

Denis O'Hempsey was buried in the cemetery at St Aiden's church in Magilligan. A stone monument was erected in his honour in the walled garden in Garvagh, where he had his first harp lessons from Brigid O'Cahan. His famous Downhill harp is exhibited in the Guinness Museum in Dublin. A poem inscribed on its side explains the origin of the bog fir:

In the time of Noah I was green.
Since the flood I have not been seen
Until seventeen hundred and two I was found
By C.R. O'Kelly underground.
He raised me up to that degree
Queen of music you may call me.

Swansong

By Michelle McCartney

Never loved that song 'Danny Boy',
too sad – too much like death and
Siobhan McKenna for me.
A swan song droned by too many sean-nós

Until he took me by surprise from his
death bed, as morphine leached
away his spirit. For a while we'd sung:
not sure if he was
there inside that subsiding shell.

Songs he'd sung and
verses we loved ourselves
Anything to reach into him
And then he did it,

No more than a drone; he hummed
'Danny Boy'. His last stand.
The chords, a wisp of the fine
voice that once was there.

Just a mumble but,
as was his custom
he raised his finger to help him
climb the scale before his final ascent.

And we knew he was there then.
His last generous act to let us know of his
acceptance of our humble gifts to him
of love and the bitter sweet depth of our sorrow.

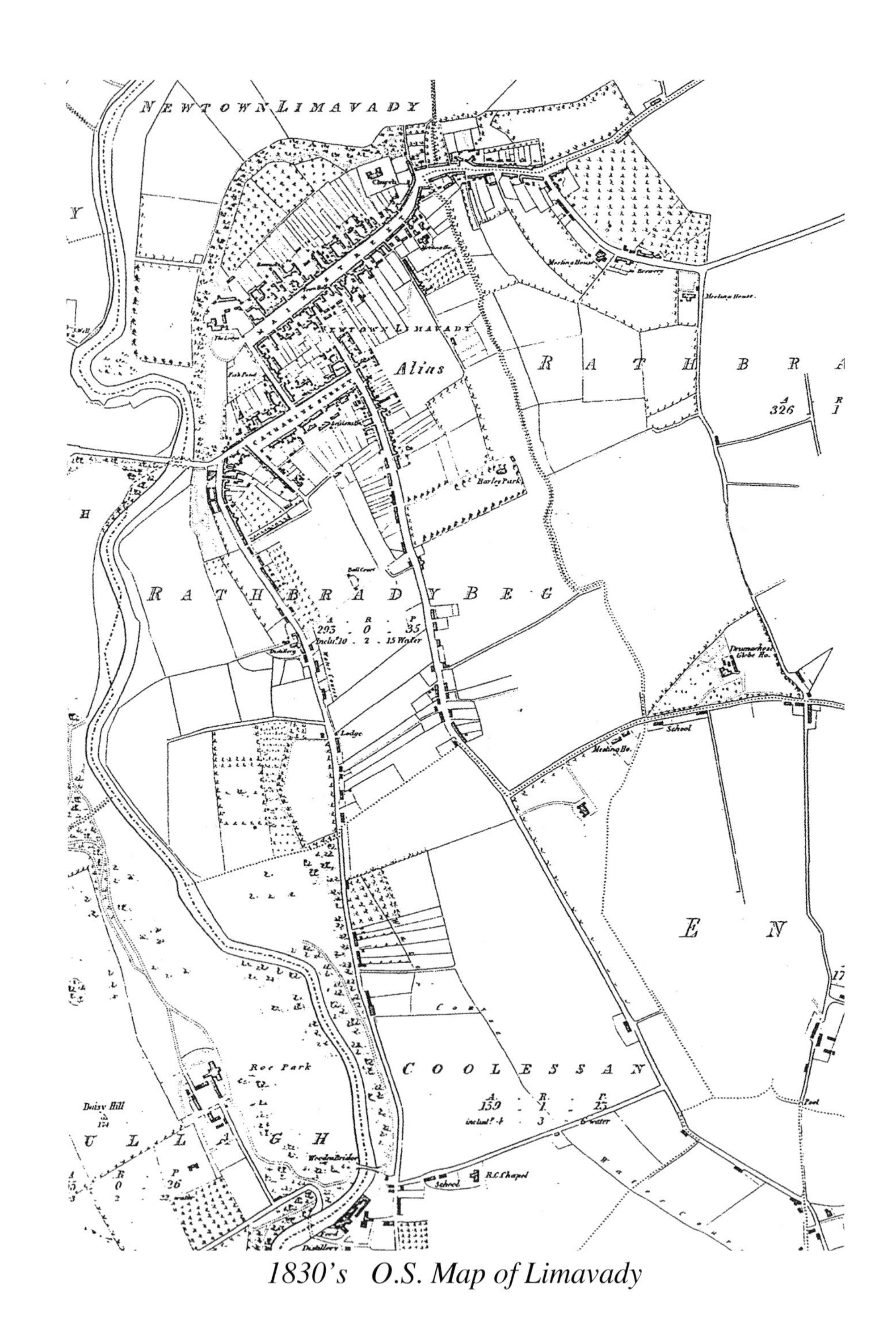

1830's O.S. Map of Limavady

Danny Boy
Part Three

George Petrie

(Dublin - Early 1830s)

George Petrie was in a right grumpy mood. He had put his heart and soul into his latest art exhibition and knew it was his best work to date. The critics however, did not like his paintings, calling them old-fashioned and romantic. 'They can all go hang. They think that painting with oils is superior: I'm going to stick to watercolours, no matter what they say!' he shouted - at nobody in particular.

He needed to get out of Dublin, do a bit of writing. It was a few years since his book on the round towers of Ireland had been published. His colleagues at the Royal Irish Academy enjoyed teasing him about his nickname: The Father of Archaeology.

A young servant girl raced into his study, letting the door bang behind her.

'Is the house on fire, Alice?'

'No, yer honour. Dis letter's only after arrivin' for you!' she gasped breathlessly.

'How many times have I told you to knock first?'

'Oh, I'm forgettin' me manners. It's from Colonel Colby. I do be thinkin' it might be trouble. His man's all of a tizzy. Said he was for goin' to Ulster. God bless us all. Do you think it's another risin'? Beggin' your pardon, your honour, sir.'

'Thank you, Alice. You may rest assured it's not another rising.'

George was delighted with the contents of the letter.

Three nights later George arrived in Newtownlimavady (Limavady). The Roe salmon which was served to him was the best he had ever tasted; potatoes were big balls of flour, oozing with salty butter and scallions. In the morning a big fry of bacon, kidneys, eggs and black pudding really set him up for the day. He rubbed his back, sore from the jolts and bumps of badly rutted roads. The journey from Dublin had taken longer than he had expected – three whole days. George was keen to get started.

George's job was to assist the army with the drawing of the first Ordinance Survey map of the whole island of Ireland – starting at Magilligan and including every town, village, hamlet, townland, mountain, river and lake. George led a team of scholars charged with the task of writing the Ordinance Survey Memoirs to go with the map. The countryside around Limavady was exceptionally beautiful; he planned to paint landscapes of the River Roe and of Binevenagh, if there was time to spare.

George's job would take him around the countryside, talking to people, recording their memoirs, describing their homes and ways of life, as well as recording discoveries of ancient monuments and artefacts. Old ways of living were changing rapidly: there were railways in England and it would only be a matter of time before Ireland had them too. Work had begun on the construction of a railway line between Dublin and Kingstown (now called Dun Laoghaire). It was a very exciting time to be alive.

The congregation in Limavady's Christ Church took a good look at the stranger. 'How much do you bet, he's with the mapmakers?' Canon Crawford overheard one of his parishioners say.

'A good Christian man should not be making bets,' remarked the canon. The mortified man hurried away.

The canon introduced George Petrie to some members of the congregation, including the Ross family who owned vast tracts of land in the Roe Valley, and lived just up the street from the church: 'I believe you have much more in common with this Irishman than with any of your Scottish ancestors. Mr Petrie is here to work with the Ordinance Survey people. He is quite a famous artist, travel writer and archaeologist, to mention but a few of his talents.' He left them to chat.

George became a frequent visitor at 51 Main Street in the town. Jane Ross, her sisters and brother William, entertained him with their singing and piano-playing; they talked for hours about music and art. George told them of his plans to edit a music magazine called The Dublin Penny Journal: he planned to collect and publish ancient music of Ireland.

After dinner every Sunday, rain or shine, with an easel under his arm George headed off towards the woods, getting many a strange look from locals who wondered at a gentleman spending Sunday afternoons ankle-deep in mud by the River Roe. 'You're wastin' your time with that paintin'. It's fishin' you should be at. Don't you know the Roe is teemin' with salmon and sea trout?' called a weather-beaten fisherman, bent over his rod like a battered old eagle.

George wondered how he could possibly do justice to the scene before him: bluebells seeped and flowed around his feet, the lower trunks of awakening trees shadowed by a blue tide. Red-coated squirrels frolicked in spreading branches high above. The air was filled with songs of blackbirds and thrushes. Barely making a splash, an otter slid into water.

All too soon George Petrie's time in Limavady came to an end. Before he left, Jane Ross called at his hotel; from her bag she took the parting gift she had been preparing for him.

'Ah, Jane, a portfolio of tunes – and all from Ulster! These will definitely grace my magazine. You can be my ears in the northwest. Promise me that if you come across any musical gems you will send them to me. Remember: if a song touches the heart, it is a good song that must not be lost.'

George was delighted with the numerous old churches, holy wells and ancient standing stones which he had recorded in the parishes of Drumachose and Tamlaghfinlagan. He was amazed by the number of Viking pots that had been unearthed in fields around Glack and The Largy. He never forgot the hospitality he had received from Jane and her family.

Jane Ross sent Irish airs to George Petrie, but it was more than a dozen years before she found a gem the likes of which George was seeking. In 1851, after hearing Jimmy McCurry playing O'Cathain's Lament outside her house, Jane, remembering George's parting words, wrote down the music and posted it to Dublin.

George was absolutely thrilled: at last he had discovered a melody with power to touch the soul. He named the tune The Londonderry Air and published it in 1855 in a collection called The Ancient Music of Ireland . Soon it became popular in London, as well as in Dublin, and was played at parties in fashionable homes. Some prim Victorian Londoners objected to the title because it sounded too much like derriére (a French word for buttocks); they called it The Air from County Derry. Many different lyrics which were written for it, including In Derry Vale and Emer's Farewell, did not catch on.

George Petrie was more than pleased with the part he played in the preservation of The Londonderry Air.

On Danny Boy

(In memory of my mother)

by *Deirdre Devine*

Oh Danny Boy, I hear her soaring voice,
I see her curling auburn hair, her green eyes
thrust to Heaven as she sings: the pipes
are calling, over glens, down mountainsides;
her audience enthralled as she performs
on stage, in a smoke-filled, hotel functions room.

The summer's gone when she would entertain,
her voice filling the air with strength and swell.
Blue flowers have recently died on her grave;
six summers of good growing made them bloom.
Snow will whiten valleys soon, as Christmas
beckons. I still hear the sound she made,

the stir her voice once raised: soft, full and
resonant; then loud, and louder yet.
We'd lower our eyes and worry over the
last lines of Danny Boy. Would she make it?
She raised roofs, while the basic amplifier
did no justice to her trained soprano voice.

She did not need it, but refused to be
without my father's new technology.
On stage, she proudly held the microphone,

preferring nightly audience rapport to being
at a cooker making meals. She would grace the
small arena of her uncle's kitchen, willingly,

with Gounod's Ave Maria. Unaccompanied at a
graveside, or in the loneliness of the chapel, a local
funeral gathering would be treated to Amazing Grace.
Her sacred notes of Panis Angelicus made wedding
congregations smile, and weep. She often said
she didn't care what she would ever lose,

as long as it would never be her voice. I asked
her once what her ambition was. To go to Heaven,
she had simply said. I pray that I will hear her there,
one day. Whenever Danny Boy is sung, I sing along,
and though I know my alto voice may not sound the
same, in my mind, I am singing as she sang.

Photograph of Main Street Limavady.

Danny Boy
Part Four

(Main St. Limavady 2010)

As I make my way to Christ Church in Limavady, the dying sun casts blood-red rays across the darkening Halloween sky. Batman, Red Riding Hood, monsters and ladybirds leap excitedly in the queue for burgers and chips at McNulty's. Sudden eddies of dried leaves, like wizened skulls, swirl around my feet.

In the nearby cemetery the grave I seek is on the left of the path: Jane Ross born 1810 died 1879. A plain concrete headstone, larger than some; nothing written on it refers to her part in passing down the Danny Boy air. I see the stained glass church window which she donated. Shivering in the evening chill I stand at Jane's graveside and wonder about her life in nineteenth century Limavady.

This is the story of the part played by Jane Ross and Jimmy McCurry in giving the world-famous air its roots in this northern market town.

Jane Ross and Jimmy McCurry (1851)

51 Main Street, Limavady

Jane Ross used a jewelled silver pin to secure a knot of hair at the nape of her neck, then rushed down the stairs. Her father scowled at her over his glasses because, as usual, Jane was last to take her place at the breakfast table. From behind the Ulster Gazette, John Ross, a stickler for time, started his usual rant: 'Jane, I don't know how often I've told you about your timekeeping! It's up to us to set a good example; otherwise the servants will do what they like. Elizabeth, Caroline and William are always punctual. There's no excuse for tardiness.'

'Sorry, Papa. I will try harder.'

The Ross family tucked into bowls of thick porridge followed by bacon, mushrooms, eggs and hot soda farls lathered with melting churned butter. The large oak dining table was set with a white linen tablecloth and fine bone china. A silver bowl of white roses marked the centre.

'I see the potato harvest has been good again. That's two consecutive years now since the blight, thanks be to the good Lord. That will mean less work for you girls with the poor, you'll be pleased to hear. Now you can get back to your art, embroidery and music.'

The sisters smiled ruefully at each other. They had enjoyed their charity work during the Great Famine. It gave purpose to their lives, made them feel better about the food they enjoyed while so many of the poor died in the workhouse, or even by the roadsides, their mouths stained green from eating grass. Many country people had left for the New World.

Jane often thanked God that her family had been blessed. She wondered how the emigrants felt, arriving in America with nothing but the clothes they wore. Her ancestors had come from Scotland, during the Plantation of Ulster, and were given a good parcel of land which had belonged to the O'Cathains.

Jane, like others from her church, did her best to help the poor and the destitute. Suitable husbands had not been found for any of the Ross girls, so they lived as upper-class spinsters, dependant on their father and brother for almost everything. Jane gave music lessons to children of the parish and she played the organ at church every Sunday.

One particular morning, exasperated by a pupil's almost tone-deaf piano playing, Jane pulled back the drapes and looked out on the usual hustle and bustle of market day on Main Street. Across the street, in bright morning sunshine, farmers' carts were parked in a long row, shafts resting on the ground. On the opposite side farmers stood around in groups, haggling over prices. When agreement was reached they spat on their hands before shaking to seal the deals – handshakes were as good as cheques.

A row of canvas stalls had been erected and hawkers were selling all sorts of things: clothes-pegs, tin cups, buckets, hazel baskets,

milking stools, tea sets, pottery – everything from a needle to an anchor, they boasted. Jane could hear the songs of caged larks; they were popular among rich folk. She had often heard them ridicule the poor for eating larks during the famine yet there they were, buying them for the novelty.
Immediately across from her house was the Burns & Laird Shipping Office. As was usual on market day, a young blind fiddler was preparing to play between the shafts of an orange and blue cart, his upturned hat on the ground to collect donations. The last few years' semi-starvation had been hard on him.

Jane opened the window to catch a breath of fresh air, but there was a strong whiff of manure from the street below. She was just about to shut it again when she heard the opening strains of a beautiful tune being played on a violin. She remained transfixed at the window, mesmerised by the haunting melody. She wanted to cage it, learn it, share it with the world.

Hurriedly Jane dismissed her pupil, changed into a dark outdoor dress and grabbed a piece of paper and a pencil. She rushed outside, held her fitted skirts high above the dirt of the street and crossed over to the young fiddler.

***

Jimmy McCurry had music in his blood; on Islay, an island off the west coast of Scotland, his people were once bards to the Lords of the Isles. The McCurrys, unlike the Rosses, had not

been gifted lands by the government. John McCurry, his father, had fallen in love with a Ballycastle beauty on one of his many trips to North Antrim. They had married and moved to Myroe, near Limavady, where Jimmy had been born.
Like Denis O'Hempsey and Rory Dall O'Cathain before him, Jimmy had contracted smallpox as a child and had survived, but it had left the mark of blindness upon him. His grandfather's fiddle, which had been kept in the rafters, was brought down when Jimmy was big enough to hold it and wield the bow. The bridge had fallen away, the catgut had snapped but the wood's smooth rounded feel and the rosin's rich oily smell totally captivated the boy. The fiddle was mended and Jimmy began his career as a fiddler and storyteller.

Jimmy was a bright lad with a wicked sense of humour and he soon learned all the old tunes from the Roe Valley area. Some melodies had been around since, and even before, the days of the O'Cathains. Jimmy composed many tunes including The Maid of Carrowclare, The Star of Moville, The Coleraine Regatta and Sarah Jane, all of which can still be heard to this day.

One golden autumn day after Jimmy had tuned the fiddle, in his usual place between the shafts of a cart outside the Shipping Office in Main Street, he played a tune he had learned from an old Magilligan fiddler. Some said that O'Hempsey, the last great bard, had rarely played it, having a strange notion that the tune had been stolen from faeries. He was afraid of their anger. Young Jimmy was not superstitious: the evocative lament was part of his repertoire. Jimmy played with his heart and soul, remembering losses he had experienced in his twenty-one years, particularly of his eyesight. He had only a dim recollection of the bright beautiful world which was lost to him forever when he was only three years old.

As the final notes faded, Jimmy heard the clack of a well-heeled lady approaching. He bowed low, then smiled, in hope of a request.

'What is that tune you were playing just now?' the lady enquired.

Jimmy shook his head. 'Ach a dinnay know, but it's as aul' as the air we breathe, ma'am.'

She asked him to repeat it several times, while she wrote down the notes. Jimmy was only too pleased to oblige.

When she had finished writing she gave Jimmy a coin which he immediately put in his mouth – to find out its value. Surprised by the feel of a florin, instead of the usual penny, Jimmy called after her, 'Ma'am! You ha'e made a mistake. That's a two bob bit you gave me!'

'No mistake, my good man. It's worth every farthing.'

Jimmy wished that every day could be as rewarding: he had enough to spare for a drink or two that evening – a rare treat.

***

Jane Ross was happy with the events of the day. The melody she had obtained from the blind fiddler was one that she had never heard before. Sitting at a carved wooden desk in her first floor drawing room, she wrote a letter to her friend George Petrie in Dublin, and sent him a copy of the music. She had met George about fifteen years earlier, when he had been in Limavady to collect information for the very first detailed map of the whole province. He was also a collector and publisher of ancient Irish music; Jane was hopeful that the ancient air she had discovered would be worthy of inclusion in one of his famous Dublin music magazines. It was very exciting.

Jane turned her mind to church matters: her brother, now Canon William, had asked her to buy a new chalice and paten for Christ Church. She could imagine his delight when he would see them. She had acquired a real bargain – money was scarce everywhere and nobody was buying silver.

The lives of the inhabitants of Limavady were improving. Famine would soon be a distant memory and people could begin to enjoy finer things such as music, dancing and poetry.

Photo by Herbert Lambert, Bath

Fred. E. Weatherly

Bringing Danny Boy Back Home
Part Five

(From 1912 to present day)

Willy John Stewart stretched and groaned. His seventy-three year old body ached from years of working in gold mines. Even though the day was almost done, the Colorado sun warmed his bald head. This was the time of day that Willy John liked best, when the miners had finished work. The mine women sat in groups, knitting or sewing quilts from scraps of old clothes. After a meal of yellow maize, dried fish and beans, the men emerged into dying light to relax and listen to the young fiddler who had just begun to play, under the pine trees.

'What about a game of whist, Willy John? I'll beat you the night.'

'You will, my eye!' laughed Willy John, pulling up a stool to join them. He knew all the old tunes having been a fine fiddler himself, before rocks had come tumbling down on top of him in a mine, crushing his arm, rendering it useless. That was the only reason he had been allowed to stay on in a cabin that was meant to house only working men. He had nowhere else to go: no family of his own. These workers' fathers and uncles had been his friends, closer even than family; together they had left the Roe Valley in Ulster, when they were youngsters of eight or nine.

‘Would you mind if we join you?’
A woman’s voice was behind him. It was unusual to have a well-educated woman at the camp. The men widened the circle to include her and her companion. She introduced herself as Margaret and her husband as Dr. Edward Weatherly.

‘Like yourselves, my husband and I came here with wild dreams of making our fortunes. We were working on the far side of the mountain but it’s become crowded and dangerous. The music attracted us to your camp. Such a strange and haunting air; the looks of loss on the faces of the men gathered round really moved me. What’s the name of that tune?’

‘Different people call it different names. Some called it O’Catháin’s Lament and then there are others that call it Aisling an Óigfear. It’s an old Irish tune that was played in my hometown, Limavady.’

‘Was it the gold rush that brought you all so far from home?’ Margaret asked kindly, seeing tears gather in the old man’s eyes as he spoke of Limavady.

‘Well, it was and it wasn’t. The Great Famine brought me to Boston as a lad. Then, around the turn of the century, work began to get scarce so we headed west, with everyone else, as part of the gold rush. I’d have been better off if I’d stayed in Boston.’ Willy John pointed at his withered limb.

‘Tell me about the famine in Ireland. Was it very bad?’

‘I wouldn’t call it bad: it was worse than that. It was hell on earth. I’m glad that I’m here in America; I never had a day’s hunger since I got here in 1847. I don’t remember much about the old country for I was only a cub when I came to America.

'In Ireland, we had a few acres rented from the land agent. We had a cow. A big red and white cow called Sally. She would just stand by the wooden gate and stare at you with her big wise eyes. We had hens too. My father, I hope he's happy in heaven, grew potatoes, big ones called lumpers. What we didn't eat, we sold to pay the rent and buy a few odds and ends. I remember us all round the fire, my brother Andy and the baby, wee Sadie, with bowls of floury potatoes on our knees and big mugs of buttermilk. Them were happy days – the best days of my life.

'Then, one August, we awoke to a terrible stink. I remember opening the door and there was a mist as thick as an aul' grey blanket, and that stench seeping into the very stones of the house. My poor father came in, mucked to the elbows, with a handful of rotten potatoes in his hands. He flung them into the fire. They sizzled and spat. Then he sat down at the table and wept. It's not good for a boy to see his father cry.

' "It's the blight!" he cried. "Half of the crop is destroyed! What's to become of us?"

'I remember, like it was yesterday, my mother putting her arms around him saying, "Sure we never died a winter yet. We'll get by with the help of God."

'She thought that the reason for the blight was that there weren't enough prayers being said. We vowed to double our praying. That first year of the blight we nearly wore out the pages of the Bible with all our reading and praying and singing of the psalms. Others said it was the work of the devil.

'Then, in the spring, we had to sell the cow to buy seed potatoes. We put in the lumpers again, for they were usually a great crop. The same thing happened a second time, at the tail end of the summer. If I close my eyes I can still smell the rot. Then our wee Sadie got sick and died.

'My uncle and aunt and cousins hadn't a bite to eat so they ended up in Limavady workhouse. There the family was all split up. It was a shameful place to be in. Next, my wee brother, Andy, got the fever too. Famine fever, they called it. We buried him alongside the baby and it broke my mother's heart. She was never right after that.

'So we upped sticks and came to America, along with thousands of other Irish families – or what was left of families. Och, I'll never forget that aul' boat with all its rolling and rocking and the reek of so many people all squashed in, tight as fish in a barrel. I thought the journey would never end. There was nothing but sea and sky all around us. It was a great day when we spied land.

'My father got a job digging the railroads. He worked with a pickaxe alongside men that he had known back home in Ulster. Two million Irish people settled in America in the 1840s alone. My mother just sat in the rooms we rented and cried most of the time. Young and all as I was, I got work as a messenger boy. I got to know the streets of Boston as well as I knew the mountains and valleys around Limavady.

'I'm sorry, ma'am. I must be boring you with all my reminisences. It's a long time since I spoke about the past.'

'Quite the contrary, sir. I find your story fascinating. But tell me about that beautiful tune the fiddler was playing when we arrived.

Do you think he could play it again for me?'

The fiddler was only too happy to play for the American lady and the English doctor. She took a notebook from her pocket and wrote down the tune. 'It's for Fred, my brother-in-law, who lives in the beautiful old city of Bath, in Somerset, England. He collects music and writes lyrics. Not what you would expect from a lawyer. I do believe he has written over a thousand songs – he sure will be able to put some fine words to this tune.'

Margaret Weatherly and her husband bade the men goodnight and moved off into the darkening light. Willy John Stewart had not had such a captive audience since before the accident, when he had played all his beloved Irish airs on his fiddle.

***

In Bath Fred Weatherly glanced at the mail his secretary had just left on his desk: nothing urgent. He placed the legal letters in a drawer and tore open a battered looking envelope. A wide smile lit up his face: this one was from Margaret, his American sister-in-law. He liked her fresh way of writing. She wrote just as she spoke, in short quick sentences, flitting from one subject to another.

Sun beamed down on the ancient Roman city. It was too good a day to stay indoors. Stuffing the letter into his pocket, Fred flew down the stairs and out the door, not stopping till he reached the banks of the River Avon. He sat under a large chestnut tree,

reading Margaret's letter with news of his brother, the fool who had given up medicine to go searching for gold. She described their hardships in the gold mines in Ouray. She also told of Limavady miners and fiddle music that entranced her, under the Colorado stars.
A sudden breeze caught the last page of the letter and whipped it up in the air. Fred just managed to catch it before it blew into the river. Written in pencil was the tune she had got from a Limavady fiddler in Colorado. Fred scanned the page, hummed, his heart began to race – 'It almost fits Danny Boy!' He sang it all the way home.

Rifling through his mountain of song sheets Fred found what he was seeking – the lyrics for a song called Danny Boy which he had written several years earlier; he had never been able to find a tune to go with the words. Now he had the tune as well as the lyrics. With a few little changes here and there, Danny Boy was born.

It became a favourite song at concerts and in the homes of anyone with a piano, a fiddle or a mouth organ. Just a few years earlier Emil Berliner, a German immigrant in America, invented the gramophone. This meant that, for the first time, those who could not play instruments were able to listen to music of their choice in their own homes. Fred wondered about such a beautiful tune coming from Ulster, where there was so much strife between the native Irish and the Ulster Scots. They were forever fighting.

In Fred's autobiography he said he hoped that both traditions would sing this song together. His hopes have come true: Danny Boy has become a shared symbol of belonging, accepted by all traditions. The song has been recorded over two hundred times and in many different languages. Elvis Presley said it was a tune written by angels. It has been downloaded to I-Pods all over the world.

In Catherine Street, Limavady, just across from Hunter's café, is The Jane Ross Commemoration Sculpture and water fountain, designed and made by Philip Flanagan, the internationally acclaimed Belfast artist and sculptor. Everyone in Limavady has his or her own opinion about the sculpture - that is the great thing about art. I love the sculpture's energy and fluidity which, to me, represents the nature of the Danny Boy air.

Over twenty years ago I heard Danny Boy being played in the Quincy Market in Boston. I felt a lump in my throat, my eyes brimmed with tears and I had an overwhelming longing to return to home to Ireland.

One year later I was boarding a Dublin bound Aer Lingus plane at Logan Airport with a one-way ticket in my hand. Danny Boy had called me back to Limavady, where Rory Dall O'Cathain, Denis O'Hempsey and Jimmy McCurry had played it, and Jane Ross had written it down, all those years ago.

Famine Emigration

(Thoughts of a twelve year old)

By Paul Hayward

Hungry, distraught, they board the ship
Gaze at the shore with trembling lip.
This will be jail for a month or so.
Wonder should they stay or should they go.

Rat infested ship sails from the dock
Rough waves make all things rock.
Rats scurry and scamper, gnawing on bones.
Listen hard, you may hear ghostly groans.

The captain yells, 'Land ahoy!'
Survivors are filled with great joy.
In America they get the lowly jobs.
Missing all at home, everyone sobs.

Migrants become servants and slaves,
Glad to avoid the watery graves.
Now the Irish have started again.
There is no famine; there is food for all men.

Children's Skipping Song (1840's)

(Author unknown)

Limavady has a workhouse, a workhouse, a workhouse
Limavady has a workhouse
Nobody wants to go in.

Don't go into the workhouse, the workhouse, the workhouse
Don't go into the workhouse
You'll never get out again.

Life is hard in the workhouse, the workhouse, the workhouse
Life is hard in the workhouse
You work from dawn to ten.

Nothing to eat but Peel's brimstone, brimstone, brimstone
Nothing to eat but Peel's brimstone
For breakfast, dinner and tea.

Limavady has a workhouse, a workhouse, a workhouse
Limavady has a workhouse
Nobody wants to go in.

The Broighter Gold

(1896)

Joseph Gibson folded his newspaper. The article on the benefits of double-ploughing cheered him no end. He had wondered why the yield of barley had been so disappointing the previous year. After all, Broighter land, by the banks of Lough Foyle was rich and fertile. He would get his men to hitch up the horses to both ploughs and double-dig the field in readiness for the coming year's turnip crop.

So it was, on an icy February day in 1896, Joseph Gibson sent two of his workers, Tom Nicholl and James Morrow, to double-plough one of his many fields: James ploughed a furrow, closely followed by Tom with another plough set to dig at a deeper level.

Tom and James worked hard and tried to withstand biting wind blowing in from the Lough. Damp clay stuck to the ploughmen's leaden boots. Flocks of gulls and crows followed in their wake, swooping and feasting on worms and beetles the ploughshares had overturned.

Wind carried harsh cries of Brent geese feeding on mud flats on the shore. Every October, Tom and James competed to see who would be first to hear honking or see geese flying in V-formation as they arrived from the far frozen north of Canada and Greenland, to feed on the shores of Lough Foyle. In spring the ploughmen watched them fly north to nest and raise their young. As the year progressed, the whole cycle would begin again.

At the end of every furrow, James and Tom stamped their feet hard and slapped their arms around their bodies several times to keep warm. Ploughing was the coldest job on the farm. James could feel the north wind slice through him, making him shiver. Tom kept his head down to shield his face. The plough struck something hard.

'Another blinking stone!' muttered Tom as he stooped low to have a look, in case the plough was damaged. The obstruction was some kind of metal dish. When he removed it from the sock of the plough, Tom noticed other metal things embedded in a big clod of earth.

'Whoa there, James! Come here to you see this!' he shouted. They often found old clay pipes or broken crockery, sometimes the remains of an old boot.

'Boys a dear, Tom, what do you think it might be?' James was wide-eyed with excitement, coldness forgotten.

'You never know. We'd need to get all this muck off first.'

They abandoned ploughing and raced to the farmyard, high as kites with excitement.

Joseph, Tom and James stood around watching as Maggie, the maid, washed away layers of soil. Tom was glad of an opportunity to watch her. She was young, beautiful and set Tom's heart all a flutter.

'It's gold! Sure as God, it's gold!' Joseph gasped.

Maggie continued to remove the clay. All that was heard was running water and a ticking kitchen-clock as men held their breaths. In Maggie's hands beautiful gold ornaments emerged: a thick gold collar decorated with fancy swirls, a gold boat complete with oars and mast, a round bowl and what looked like two bracelets and two necklaces.

There was not another stroke of work done on the farm for the rest of the day; excitedly they speculated on the value and origin of their find: who had put it in the ground in the first place and why?

The next day Joseph donned his Sunday suit, polished his shoes until they shone and set off to Derry with the horse and trap. He carried the treasure wrapped in his wife's best pillowcase, which she had embroidered before their marriage.

A bell jangled above the jeweller's door as Joseph opened it. With a glass to one eye, the jeweller hemmed and hawed, tut-tutted and shook his head.

'Oh, it's damaged here. I'd need to get a specialist to clean it up. These specialists don't come cheap, you know. Might even have to take it to Dublin. I don't know if it would be worth me going to all that bother. You've heard of fool's gold, haven't you?'

Joseph could tell that he was interested, even though he pretended not to be.

‘I could take it off your hands for thirty guineas. Mind you, I could be doing myself here. Sure it could well turn out to be worth nothing.’

Joseph Gibson was nobody’s fool: he understood the gleam in the jeweller’s eye. After a lot of haggling, the jeweller counted £200 into Joseph’s hands. He could expand the farm; his wife would want new furniture. Joseph hurried to the bank to deposit the money. Thanks to the honesty of Tom and James he banked what would have taken either of them almost three years’ hard work to earn.

The jeweller was a canny man with good connections. He sold the Broighter gold to a Cork collector who, after taking the gold to Dublin for repair, discovered that the seat from the boat and a part of a torc, or collar, was missing. He travelled by train from Cork to Limavady, to search for the missing pieces.

Days of searching yielded nothing. When Maggie had been washing the gold she had not taken a great deal of care. Truth to tell, her mind was on the closeness of Tom, and him so kind and handsome. Some of the smaller sections may have been thrown away with the dirty water.

The Cork man asked dozens of questions. He had men dig up the drains in the hope of finding missing pieces. They found nothing. He had no hope of finding the seat: James discovered it in the field the day after Joseph took the hoard to Derry, gave it to his

Poetry *for Paul*

Somewhere,

In the music of your making,

Our spirits met.

A chord was shared.

A calling was fulfilled.

Your fingers pluck a tune from air.

Words play around your hair.

A song is willed again to live

And poetry is born.

Deirdre Devine

To Paul on your 21st Birthday with love

sister as a present, and she sold it to a jeweller in Limavady.

The fuss died down after a year and the ploughmen's lives returned to normality. Often as they sat on a ditch, drinking warm sweet tea from lemonade bottles corked with screwed up newspaper and eating soda farls and potato bread, they would remember the day they found the gold and wonder about its history.

The British Museum bought the Broighter gold from the Cork dealer for £600. Sir Arthur Evans, a distinguished archaeologist, wrote a long and detailed article about it in an English magazine. Local papers printed the story and hordes of strangers arrived in Broighter – hoping to find more treasure. They went away empty-handed and disappointed.

'It's getting like California around here with this gold rush!' laughed James.

When the Royal Irish Academy, whose job it was to collect and preserve objects of historical interest for future generations, found out about it, they demanded that the British Museum hand the treasure over to the Irish Museum in Dublin. Their request was flatly refused and the Academy took them to court.

The law regarding treasure-trove was very complicated. It stated that if precious objects had been lost, then finders keepers! On the other hand, if it could be proven that objects were hidden and the owner had planned to collect them later, they would be considered treasure-trove belonging to the Crown.

The British Museum put up a strong case. No one knew where the gold had originated. Experts concluded it was Celtic and about a thousand years old; they believed that the waters of the Foyle had flowed over the Broighter field at the time the treasure was deposited.

In those ancient times, before St. Patrick, Irish people revered many gods. They believed that when Manannan, the powerful sea-god, was angry, he caused great storms in the Foyle to capsize boats and bring waves inland, flooding the land. To keep the sea-god happy, they gave him generous gifts; small gifts were useless. He could cause great destruction and grief. Extravagant gifts like gold and precious stones were taken on to the Lough, in a rowing boat, and thrown overboard as offerings to placate Manannan.

The lawyers for the British Museum argued that if the gold had been thrown overboard, as a gift to the sea-god, the owners had never planned to collect it later. Hence it belonged to the finders who, in this case, had sold it. The court case dragged on and was eventually brought to the Royal Courts in London.

In 1903, seven years after the find, Tom received a very official looking letter with a London postmark. He knew no one in London. Carefully he opened it and read it twice. He could hardly take it in: he had been summoned by the Royal Court to go to London to give evidence about finding the gold. They would pay £10 to help cover his expenses.

Tom had never been as far as Dublin, never mind London. An English solicitor made all the travel arrangements. Tom took the train from Limavady Junction to Belfast and then boarded the overnight boat to Liverpool. He felt seasick and wondered how sailors put up with all the continuous motion.

When the boat docked in Liverpool Tom felt like kissing the ground. He had never seen such tall houses – some seemed to reach to the sky. His neck hurt from looking up at grand buildings. He asked a tattooed man for directions to Lime Street Station, where he had been told he would catch the London train. The man called him Paddy and spoke musically, almost like he was singing.

'My name's Tom, not Paddy,' said Tom.

'Over 'ere you're Paddy, mate!' laughed the stranger.

Tom thought he would never reach London. The landscape was mostly flat and monotonous for hundreds of miles. There were no mountains or coastlines. At Euston Station, in London, he boarded one of the new electric trams to travel to the Royal Courts.

As Tom stood in the stand, answering questions, he noticed the puzzled expressions of the lawyers and judges. After a while proceedings were stopped: they could not understand Tom's Ballykelly accent. That did not surprise Tom one bit – he was having a hard time understanding them! The court was adjourned until an interpreter was found.

The judge called an expert archaeologist who had been to Broighter to examine the place where the treasure was found. Although it was only about three feet above sea-level, during spring tides, the expert claimed that the land had been dry for well over a thousand years. On this evidence, the court decided that the Broighter gold was indeed treasure-trove. The British Museum was ordered to hand it over to King Edward VII; graciously he gave it to the Royal Irish Academy.

Tom was pleased that the Broighter gold would be returned to Ireland. He had seen many grand sights in London but was more than happy to be going home: London was so busy and noisy. He missed the wide-open spaces of home, the cries of the corncrake and curlew, and he wondered how anyone who lived in London could remain sane.

On his return he would ask Maggie McLoughlin to marry him. It would have been nice to have had Broighter Gold made into a wedding ring, but that was impossible. He had money to buy a ring from the local jeweller and enough left over to pay for the wedding, thanks to the generous expenses' payment he had received for his trip to London.

Tom and Maggie lived long and happy lives together. He never visited Dublin to see the Broighter Gold displayed in the National Museum. Tom died in the Roe Valley Hospital in 1964.

Note

There have been other similar finds of gold jewellery throughout Europe but what makes the Broighter Gold so special is the little boat. Nobody knows where the gold came from or how it ended up in a field. Sometimes it is best not to have the whole story: then we can all dream and make up our own stories.

If you ever happen to be in Dublin, be sure to call in to the National Museum of Ireland, where you can see the hoard. Just think: if Joseph Gibson had not decided to double-plough his field in 1896, that gold could still be lying below the soil, in a field in Broighter.

The Broighter Hoard

By Debbie Caulfield

It is treasure-trove, in law, if it was not lost,
if those who buried it intended to return,
dig it up, reclaim it as their own.

Trowel the surface gently to reveal
layers and layers of memories – stacked and stored
mapped recorded, planned
mind-crafted;

each remembered sight, sound, smell, touch and taste
as much a treasure to its owner as a tiny golden boat
with golden oars – handcrafted, palms for templates,
two thousand years ago.

Treasure found, stuck
in a stagnant sheuch,
down Broighter Road
under an old umbrella.

Glen to Glen

Denis Hegarty - Snowy Benbradagh

Brendan McMenamin - Ness Woods Waterfall

Stained glass window from Christchurch, Drumachose by Jason Bell

Rough Fort, Moneyrannel Road, Limavady by Jason Bell

Mortuary House Banagher

Old Priory Dungiven

O'Cahan's Rock, Limavady by Jason Bell

Banagher Glen

Broighter Gold

Binevenagh

Tamlaght Finlagan church remains

Mussenden Temple and Benone Beach

Slopes of Binevenagh and the Roe Valley

River Roe

St. Aiden's Church Magilligan

Dungiven Castle

Cushy Glen

I grew up in a rocky barren place where north Atlantic winds battered our wee house. Many a night we all feared we would end up in the middle of the ocean itself. 'The best thing about living here is that, if it doesn't kill you, it'll make you hardy,' my father used to say, when he was sober.

My brothers were almost grown men by the time I came along. The smallpox that afflicted me when I was wee left ugly scars upon my face; strangers would stare and shake their heads. I learned to be invisible. Being short was an advantage: living in such a desolate place I could hide behind low-slung whin bushes and eavesdrop on private conversations; I could sit quietly in darkened corners looking and listening in flickering fire-light, especially in the dead of winter.

My mother returned to her own folk not long after I was born. People said she had always been bad with her nerves and my birth had sent her head completely astray.

When my father was drunk he would comment on my black hair, swarthy skin and small stature: 'I dunno where we got you from, for you're no like any o' the rest o' us. You're more like the black stranger that passes on the road from Coleraine or beyond.'

I ran wild. I knew, like the back of my hand, every square inch of the hills above Limavady and Castlerock. My favourite place was the Sconce, called Dun Cetheran by the aul' folks. From its stone top, I could see the whole of the Bann Valley, Inishowen in the west and the Scottish coastline in the east. Cetheran had been a chieftain and a cousin of Cuchlainn, the Hound of Ulster.

I used to lie in the heather watching buzzards prey upon unwary rats and mice which they would tear to pieces with hooked beaks and terrible claws. I used to play at being Cetheran, slaying enemies with my broadsword.

When I was old enough, I joined the British army and received new clothes and two pairs of strong leather boots. For the first time in my life, I had a full stomach, warm clothes and boots on my feet. I ate meat every day – mutton, pork, beef, chicken, duck and fish as well. However, there was a price to pay for all this – my freedom. I had to jump every time a whistle blew. I had blisters, big as sparrows' eggs, on my feet from all the marching.

'How come you're so good with the gun, Glen?' the others would ask after I hit the target every time.

'That's for me to know and you to find out,' I answered.

They were always asking questions. Who were my folks? What did they do? Where did I hail from?

I told them nothing.

In the barracks I fell in with Kitty, the cook. Kitty was not much to look at and could swear better than any man – my kind of woman! I met her in the evenings when the other men were drinking and playing cards. Kitty and I had seen enough of alcohol to last us a lifetime, so we avoided it. Neither of us spent a single unnecessary farthing.

Along the shores of the Foyle, we would walk arm in arm and talk about the farm we would buy on the slopes of the Sconce. I would be a landowner like Cetheran. Kitty and I were not going to be 'nobodies' any more. For security, Kitty stitched money into her clothes and, by the time I was discharged from the army, we had a tidy sum.

Our dreams came true: we married and bought a wee house and a bit of land on the slopes of the Sconce. It was good being back on the mountain, answerable to no one but ourselves.

That first spring we planted beans and sowed grass-seed to have hay for winter fodder. We bought a dozen sheep, a cow and some hens.

The neighbours scoffed; one told me to my face: 'You'd need a miracle to grow anything on that stony ground, Cushy Glen!'

'You mark my words, Kitty,' I said, 'in a couple of years we'll be on the pig's back and the envy o' all o' them that looked down on us. Pure jealousy, that's all it is.'

Our good luck lasted no time at all. That first winter, the foxes ate every last hen, putting paid to Kitty's baking. Winter was long and cold. Stray dogs killed half the sheep, the rest perished in snowdrifts. It was hard to keep going.

In the spring we planted potatoes, carrots, turnips and barley but, in the thin mountain soil, weeds and rushes smothered our crops. I shot rabbits but there was little nourishment in them. We had to sell the cow. The boy who bought her knew we were desperate and robbed us blind. From him I gained the inspiration to turn to a life of crime.

First I stole an odd hen or lamb for the pot. Then I thought of a way of making money to get us away from farming on a rocky hillside in the back of beyond. I went to fairs in Coleraine to glean information: when I learned which houses were empty, I broke in and stole money and jewellery.

In the Ram's Horn pub, I overheard two aul' boys discussing Roddy Dempsey, a highwayman from Barnault, up near Loughermore. Along the Limavady mountain road, he had lain in wait for wealthy cloth-merchants and farmers coming back from Coleraine fair, laden with goods and money. His practice was always the same: he would shoot the horse to displace the rider. Then he would slit his victim's throat and help himself to the man's takings. The road became known as The Murder Hole Road.

Roddy made the mistake of spending the stolen money. He was caught and subsequently hanged in Claudy Market Square, as a lesson to anyone else who had similar ideas. I knew I could be smarter than Roddy Dempsey.

Kitty and I planned our future. There were big farms in America, with hundreds of miles of grass, called prairie land. We felt we could have a good life together there and herds of cows and horses – thousands of miles away from sneering faces around the Sconce.

When nights were drawing in, and nobody was afoot, we dug dozens of deep holes in boggy ground along the sides of The Murder Hole Road and covered them over with sticks and ferns. Kitty was as strong as a man and worked as hard.

In the Ram's Horn one night, sitting in a corner near the door with my wide-brimmed hat pulled down well over my face, sipping lemonade, looking and listening, I overheard a big farmer from the flatlands of Myroe boasting about what he had made at the fair. His pockets were bulging with money and he was buying drinks for everybody. The craic was mighty. Wee Danny Kane lifted the door from its hinges and laid it flat on the floor for the dancing of jigs.

Nobody saw me slipping out as I hurried home to fetch my old army blunderbuss and gully-knife. Kitty came with me: an extra pair of eyes and ears. We did not feel the cold as we lay in wait, well hidden behind holly bushes, on the side of the mountain road. My heart was fairly pounding when we heard hooves clip-clop. To steady myself, I thought of the big grasslands of Oklahoma and took aim. The horse went down straight away. Before the intoxicated farmer could even begin to struggle to his feet, I had his throat cut.

'Did you get him, Cushy?'

'Aye, I did, Kitty. Oklahoma, here we come!'

The road was lonely and quiet. Carefully we took cash from his pockets and saddlebags; Kitty packed it into an old meal bag. I dragged the body in to one of the holes we had dug and used sticks and ferns to cover it. It took all my strength: making a good living on the fertile land around Myroe, he had become fat and heavy.

'May God have mercy on his oul greedy well-fed soul,' Kitty prayed blasphemously. Then we ran home in the moonlight.

I went to bed but could not sleep for excitement. Kitty sat up all night sewing a patchwork quilt by candlelight. She stitched gold sovereigns into squares of the quilt – our own secret bank.

Kitty and I lay low and carried on scraping a living. I overheard one of the neighbours telling his wife, 'The Glens could get by on the clippin's o' tin'.

Each time I killed a man it was easier than before. The takings were not always great but there was no rush. We bided our time and struck only when conditions were right. Nobody noticed me creeping around dark corners wearing my old army coat and hat. I spoke to no one and listened carefully: army training had come in handy.

One morning John McCrea, a famous tory hunter, came to our door. We were sure we had been discovered. I thought Kitty was going to have a fit, she laughed so much, as McCrea trotted back down our lane. He had come to enlist my help in tracking down highwaymen. I was to be well paid for my work. I knew every highwayman operating on the road between Coleraine and Limavady but not one of them knew me.

Before the week was out I led McCrea to Charlie Fowler's pub, outside Dungiven, where James Swann and his highwaymen were drinking and plotting in a back room. I watched the shoot-out from behind a whin bush. Swann from Limavady was arrested, tried, found guilty and hanged in Coleraine.

I was glad to see the back of my competitors but their demise meant we had to lie low longer than planned, before our last raid: one more would be enough to start our new lives. Kitty and I had lost count of the bodies we had buried: she guessed it was nearly a score.

The quilt was heavy; she had to keep gathering wool to pad it out and cover bulky jewellery and gold sovereigns. We agreed that if either of us was to be caught, or killed, the other would take the quilt and head for America. However, we felt confident that would never happen: we were invincible!

I had my eye on Harry Jim Hopkins, a big well-to-do cloth merchant from Bolea. One evening he was in a tavern in Coleraine bumming and blowing about the money he had just made at the fair and that he was not afraid to be travelling alone on The Murder Hole Road – he feared neither man nor beast. I decided his death would be my last strike: Hopkins would be an easy target because he was drunk.

Kitty and I were in great spirits.
 'Here he comes, Cushy. Sure it'll be like taking sweets from a baby by the cut of him,' Kitty giggled.

I aimed at the horse and shot it straight through the heart. I whipped out my knife to cut his throat when I heard a bang, felt a tearing pain in my chest…

Note
Harry Jim Hopkins shot Cushy Glenn dead in 1804. Neither Kitty Glen nor the stolen property was ever found. Twenty shallow graves were discovered along The Murder Hole Road. Cushy Glen was one of about six highwaymen who robbed and killed on that road, in the late seventeen and early eighteen hundreds.

Many people claim to have seen strange moving lights near the Sconce. Could the area be haunted by Cushy Glen? Or by his innocent victims? Is the phenomenon caused by marsh gas rising from the boggy ground?

In recent years, Coleraine and Limavady Borough Councils decided to change the name of the road. Although now officially known as Windy Hill, many people still call it The Murder Hole Road.

Lig Na Péiste

(Banagher, Co. Londonderry)

Saint Murrough lived in the townland of Banagher, on the Magheramore Road, over a thousand years ago. One morning he stood at the front door of his cottage watching sunrise paint the horizon pink. To his left, on higher ground, was an old timber church in a sorry-looking state. Centuries of wind and rain had necessitated many replacements of original wood, since St Patrick had first built it in 474 AD.

In his mind's eye, Murrough O'Heaney could see a lovely new stone-built church. He wondered to himself, should the new place of worship be built on low sheltered ground, where there would be easy access for the young, old and disabled people of the locality? Or should it be built on the same spot: on high ground nearer to heaven? Murrough was undecided.

Saint Patrick had arrived in Ireland by boat, to convert the people to Christianity. The pagan Irish had been worshipping all sorts of gods: mountaintops, animals – even fire. Their gods had demanded human and animal sacrifices. Many old pagan practices persisted: some people worshipped Lug, the sun god. Saint Murrough told them that they should look only to the one true God for guidance but, when God did not answer their prayers, many reverted to old pagan ways.

Standing at his cottage door, praying for wisdom, Murrough saw a stag leap over a hedge, stop for a moment, and then lope up the mountain. The stag stopped at a rock and stared straight down at him. Was this a sign from God telling him to build the new church on the original site, or was he no better than the pagans?

Saint Murrough went down on his knees, on cold bare rock, and prayed for guidance. Suddenly there was a flap of wings and a loud whoosh above his head: a golden eagle, a rock in its claw, flew over Murrough's cottage and dropped the rock on the old church. Murrough saw this as a sign: there was the place to build the new house of God.

Murrough was sitting by the fire eating a big bowl of porridge, sweetened with honey that had been a present from a neighbour, when there came a loud rapping on his door. A small agitated man stood there, running his hands distractedly through his hair.

'Your Christianity is nothing more than a great big fraud! You told us that Saint Patrick had rid Ireland of snakes and monsters. Only last week all my sheep were eaten! And what do I find today? My fields of corn burnt to a cinder and that monster snake, Lig Na Péiste, laughing his head off up there at Banagher Lake! You are our holy man. What are you going to do about it?'

'Saint Patrick rid Ireland of the snakes and monsters of paganism. I'll see what I can do, with the help of the one true God.'

Somewhat calmed, the man strode back up the hillside.

Saint Murrough was in a right quandary. He sometimes wished he was a farmer and not expected to have all the answers regarding religion. Saint Patrick was long gone, so it was up to him to advise the people. The problem with Lig Na Péiste was going to be a difficult one to solve but Murrough knew that nothing is impossible with God.

Lig Na Péiste was a snake monstrosity: eleven feet long, thick horns curled like a black-faced mountain ram's, scales on his back as big as dinner plates, a thick black tongue and poisonous venom that sent shivers up the spines of the bravest warriors. He could swallow animals whole and breathed fire that set homes and crops alight. His flaming breath's rotten smell withered the heather. He spoke fluent Irish – an evil monster left over from the beginning of time.

Murrough realised he needed to pray but it was not easy for him to concentrate: neighbours were always looking for help. He set off up the hill to where the stag had stood and the eagle had dropped the rock.

Alone, he spent eleven days in the mountains; eating berries, drinking water from streams, praying for God's protection from Lig Na Péiste and for help to rid Ireland of its last serpent.

Saint Murrough loved being on the mountainside, feasting his eyes on the wide sweep of Benbradagh and the lush lands below. He lay in the grass listening to skylarks' water-babble music and grasshoppers' humming. In the evenings he watched the sun's golden halo in the sky. The moon poured light on him, as white and bright and pure as a field of snow; he felt caressed and strengthened by the hand of God.

On the dawn of the eleventh day Murrough awoke to the shrill clear warbling of blackbirds and wrens. He knew what to do. Calmly he plucked three reeds from the bog that surrounded him and headed off to Owenreagh Burn, Lig Na Péiste's favourite place.

On a rock, the snake was curled like a coil of thick rope. Murrough covered his mouth and nose to avoid the awful stench as the serpent unwound its great long body, straight up in the air. Every bird and animal disappeared. Both were silent. The ground beneath him trembled but Murrough stood firm and still, waiting for the monster to speak.

'You're a very noble and welcome sacrifice. I will relish every single morsel of your body!' Lig Na Péiste's fangs darted back and forth as he spoke.

'Before you eat me,' said Murrough, 'because I am a holy man, I need to perform an ancient religious ritual.'

'As long as it's quick!' snapped Lig. 'I'm starving!'

'First I need you to lie down.'

With a loud slap, Lig Na Péiste flopped to the ground. Murrough placed the three reeds across the monster's back, gagging at the smell.

'Hurry up! Are you done yet?'

'Just another couple of minutes. I have to say a few prayers over you.' Murrough was praying harder than he had ever prayed in his whole life.

'All right, but only two minutes.'

As Lig Na Péiste spoke, the reeds began to grow across his body and, as they grew, they were transformed into hard metal. Soon his whole body was encased in an iron cage.

Lig Na Péiste screamed, 'You rat! You've tricked me! Release me this instant!'

'If I free you, will you promise never to harm any of God's people again?'

'I promise. Now release me! You have my word!'

Saint Murrough knew the monster could never be trusted. Lig Na Péiste writhed and thrashed about; with every move iron bonds tightened on his body.

'Let me out!' he hissed.

Murrough almost began to feel sorry for him.

'You will stay trapped until The Last Day: The Day of Judgement. Then God himself shall release you. Until that day you must live in Lough Foyle.'

'You are just a man. You can't tell me what to do!'

'Oh, Lig Na Péiste, I am only doing what God has told me to do. You are a creature of God, so you must obey!'

He gave the cage a kick and, with Lig Na Péiste firmly secured inside, the cage began to roll down the mountainside. It did not stop until it landed, with a great splash, in the cold grey waters of Lough Foyle.

Lig Na Péiste remains writhing and thrashing in his cage, trying to free himself before Judgement Day. There are dangerous tides and currents around the Tun Banks in Lough Foyle, where he lies. Over the years ships have gone down and lives have been lost there: Ireland's last serpent causes trouble on the Foyle.

After ridding himself of Lig Na Péiste, Murrough thought he would have peace to build the new church at Banagher. He was mistaken: people from all over Ireland came to him for blessings and prayers. Grateful parishioners donated money and helped build a new church which was eventually completed around the middle of the twelfth century.

Saint Murrough lived a long and holy life. Many people claimed he had cured them of diseases and worked hundreds of other miracles.

'Don't waste your time and mine coming to thank me,' he would say.

'Just get down on your knees and thank the good Lord above. Leave me in peace to study my Bible.'

Note

Saint Murrough O'Heaney is buried in a special tomb, called a mortuary house, at Banagher old church. It looks like a tiny church built of stone and, although it is hundreds of years old, it remains in perfect condition today.

At the side of the mortuary house is an opening, just big enough for a hand to enter, for the custom of sand lifting. The sand is supposed to have miraculous powers, if lifted by a descendant of Saint Murrough. If you are doing an exam, a handful of sand in your pocket is believed to guarantee good results! Before competitions jockeys used to throw sand over their racehorses, in hope of winning. Some believe the sand is powerful enough to send the devil packing!

My grandmother, when she heard some great news, used to say,
'Well, doesn't that beat Banagher?'
'And Banagher beats the devil!' was the expected reply.
I gave it with gusto every time.

The Gem Of The Roe

(Traditional song. Writer unknown.)

In a land of O'Cathain where bleak mountains rise
O'er those brown ridgy tops now the dusky clouds fly
Deep sunk in a valley a wild flower did grow
And her name was Finvola, the Gem of the Roe.

For the Isles of Abunde appeared to our view
A youth clad in tartan, it's strange but it's true
With a star on his breast and unstrung was his bow
And he sighed for Finvola the Gem of the Roe.

The Gem of the Roe, the Gem of the Roe
And he sighed for Finvola
The Gem of the Roe.

To the grey shores of Alba his bride he did bear
But short were the fond years these lovers did share
For thrice on the hillside the Banshee cried low
Twas the death of Finvola the Gem of the Roe.

The Gem of the Roe, the Gem of the Roe
Twas the death of Finvola
The Gem of the Roe.

No more up the streamlet her maidens will hie
For wan the pale cheek and bedimmed the blue eye
In silent affliction our sorrows will flow
Since gone is Finvola the Gem of the Roe.

The Gem of the Roe, the Gem of the Roe
Since gone is Finvola
The Gem of the Roe.

Finvola, the Gem of the Roe

About five hundred years ago, near the place we now call Limavady, a great chieftain named Dermot O'Cathain lived in a castle built on a rock by the swirling waters of the River Roe (nowadays known as O'Cahan's Rock.) He ruled over a vast tract of land stretching from west of Lough Foyle to the River Bann and from the Sperrins to the great rolling Atlantic at Benone. After constructing some defences around the valley, Dermot made improvements to his castle: the O'Cathains had to guard their lands from other chieftain families.

Across Lough Foyle, in Donegal, the mountains were high and the soil thin. The O'Donnell chieftain looked enviously at rich fertile land around the River Roe and wanted it for himself. He sent a band of his fiercest fighting men to the Roe Valley. In the darkness of the night they surrounded O'Cathain's castle.

Dermot awoke to find his castle encircled by the enemy. His fiercest fighters had gone on a training exercise on the far side of the river. He tried to calm his frightened wife and screaming daughter Finvola. 'Sure those barbarians could never beat the great O'Cathains! I'm playing a waiting game with them. 'We'll take them unawares and squash them like flies! Don't you worry your heads at all.'

After about a week food and morale were running low inside the besieged castle. Dermot desperately needed his warriors' help but could not get word out to them about what had happened, until one of his men had a brainwave that saved them all from certain death: 'Why don't we send Croi-croga to alert the soldiers on the far side of the river? He's a brave wee dog and a great swimmer too. As loyal a dog as ever we owned!'

The courageous dog, with a message tucked into his collar, darted unnoticed through the O'Donnell fighters and leapt into the fast-flowing river. Exhausted, shivering with cold, Croi-croga climbed the far bank and delivered his master's crucial message to the O'Cathain training camp.

The O'Donnells were soon surrounded and sent packing back to the hills of Donegal. Thus the town got its name: Leim an mhadaidh translates as dog-leap. Over time the name was anglicised in spelling, becoming Limavady.

Dermot O'Cathain made sure that such an attack could never happen again: he ordered twelve castles to be built in key positions spread throughout his territory. He had twelve strapping sons - a castle for each and every one.

Dermot loved all his children but Finvola, his only daughter, was his heart's delight. Her hair, the colour of ripe oats, cascaded down her back in soft curls. Her eyes were blue sapphires. The local people loved Finvola and called her the gem of the Roe.

Tutors taught Finvola everything a fine lady should know. Every day her brothers galloped to the abbey in Dungiven to learn swordsmanship and battle skills while she was being educated indoors, often counting threads for tapestry. Sometimes she would stamp her feet in rage, hurl tapestry into a corner and race outside, banging big oak doors behind her. She would toss off her robes and swim in the river with the salmon, laugh aloud at the long-legged, snake-necked heron, so serious and still, standing on a rock in the river – waiting for dinner to swim past! Buzzards nested in the trees; occasionally she glimpsed a golden eagle. Sometimes she was allowed to hunt with her brothers. She loved the wind in her hair, the excitement of the chase, the wild smell of blood as they hunted hares, stags and foxes.

Freshly caught meat was roasted outdoors on a huge spit. Finvola would dress up for the feasting in one of her finest linen gowns; there would be eating, singing and dancing under the stars, until dawn light glowed around Benbradagh.

Occasionally Finvola and her father sailed across the sea to Scotland to visit friends. The dangers of bad weather and strong currents excited Finvola, making her feel fully alive.

On one fateful journey they were caught in a terrible storm and their boat was badly damaged. Finvola, her brother Turloughmore, and their father, had almost given up hope of ever seeing Ireland again when a rowing-boat came into view. They were rescued by a big brave highland man, dressed in tartan. Their saviour urged them to accompany him to the castle of his lord, the MacDonnell.

'MacDonnell, Lord of the Isles!' gasped O'Cathain excitedly: the MacDonnell and O'Cathain families had been friends for generations.

'Aye, sir. He'll bid ye welcome. Nay doubt aboot that.'

Sure enough, Lord MacDonnell gave them a hearty welcome. He and his family kept their Irish guests well entertained for a few weeks before their return home: rich food, sweet mead, skirling bagpipes and lively dancing set Finvola's heart aglow. She loved the wildness of the Isles: the rocks, mists swirling in from the sea and the lilting language of the people.

Angus MacDonnell, son of the chieftain, was handsome, broad shouldered, strong, fearless and completely charmed by Finvola. He had never seen anyone so lovely, lively and full of fun. They went riding on the beautiful Isle of Islay where he taught her to tell the difference between a large gull and an osprey and showed her where to look for adders. Finvola gathered great basketfuls of bilberries that grew abundantly on the hillsides and she showed the servants how to make rich dark bilberry cordial.

By the time the O'Cahans were due to go back to Ireland, Sir Angus and Finvola had fallen in love. The young couple bade each other a tearful farewell at the harbour, with promises of undying love. A strong easterly wind shortened the homeward journey.

To help pass the time until she would see Angus again, Finvola busied herself learning skills that were thought necessary to run a castle with a lot of servants. However, domestic matters did not interest her and she would frequently gallop to the top of Binn

Fhoibhne (Binevenagh) where, on a clear day, she could see the coast of Scotland.

Finvola hankered for her love. She would pluck petals from flowers sighing, 'He loves me. He loves me not.' When she learned which flowers would give her the correct answer she plucked only them and laughed at her own silliness.

One bright sunny morning as Finvola stood at the top of Binn Fhoibhne, shielding her eyes from the sun's glare, she spotted the MacDonnell flag on a boat sailing up the mouth of Lough Foyle. She shouted and leaped with joy. Her startled horse reared up and galloped all the way to Benone beach, where her father and brothers were picnicking.

By the time Finvola reached them she was hot, footsore and dirty; Angus had landed and was running to meet her. He swung her up into his arms. 'Ach you're a sight for sore eyes!' he laughed. 'Marry me – I'll not take nay for an answer!

'I'll marry you! I'll marry you! I'll marry you!' answered the ecstatic Finvola. 'But should you not be asking my father first?'

'Aye, my wee bonnie lass, I asked him the very minute I set foot on the shore!'

There was much bargaining regarding Finvola's dowry. MacDonnell, Lord of the Isles, sent a letter to Dermot O'Cathain demanding that twenty-four young sons of the O'Cathain chieftains come and marry daughters of the MacDonnells.

Dermot took a few days to mull it over: he did not want to lose his favourite daughter and so many of his fine young relatives but, most of all, he wanted Finvola to be happy. MacDonnell would make a better friend than foe. Eventually Dermot agreed but only on condition that, after her death, Finvola's body would be returned to the Roe Valley to be buried with her own people.

On a sunny summer morning Finvola O'Cathain and Angus MacDonnell were married in the Abbey in Dungiven, under the shadow of great Binn Fhoibhne. Angus, dressed in MacDonnell tartan, cut a dashing figure. His beautiful bride wore a saffron linen gown, delicately embroidered with oak, ash and hazel leaves. A wreath of yellow buttercups crowned her head, her clear blue eyes sparkled with joy.

Dermot said a tearful goodbye to his beloved daughter. Friends and allies congratulated the happy pair and bade a final farewell to Finvola, the gem of the Roe. Then she, her new husband, twelve maids and twenty-four brave young O'Cathain men, their servants and families, set off for the Isles, leaving many a sorrowful heart behind.

Soon afterwards Dermot O'Cathain passed away. The people of the valley said he had become dispirited after Finvola sailed out through the mouth of the Foyle to make her home so far away in Islay.

Finvola and Angus lived happily until she suddenly became ill and died. Angus kept her death a secret from the O'Cathains. He could hardly believe it himself: she had been singing and dancing only a few days previously! He had her buried on the Isle of Islay and spent many hours alone, grieving by her graveside.

Turloughmore O'Cathain was out hunting stags near the top of Keady Mountain when he heard the wail of Grainne Roe O'Cathain, banshee and guardian spirit of the O'Cathains, echo down the valley from Benbradagh. Her piercing cries announced the death of an O'Cathain. He shivered. All of his father's generation were long dead. He thought of his younger brothers, already a day late returning from a sea-fishing trip. They were experienced boatmen but the waters off the north coast were treacherous.

When the brothers returned, just before dawn, Grainne Roe was still issuing doleful laments. Turloughmore sent messengers to check on the rest of the family. When news came back that all were well he realised it was Finvola, his beautiful beloved sister, who had died.

Sir Angus could see O'Cathain boats nearing the Firth. After they landed, a choir of O'Cathain women joined Grainne Roe singing a song of mourning for their cherished friend and kinswoman. They sang in praise of her beauty, virtue and noble birth, and lamented her burial among strangers.

The islanders, seeing the whole band surround the MacDonnell's burying ground, moved towards the mourners to prevent them reaching the body.

'Clear off!' warned Turloughmore with raised sword.
Seeing Sir Angus standing on a rock at the entrance, he yelled, 'Get out of my way, you dirty lying islander! Your word is worth no more than the dung of an ass!'
A fearsome highlander, brandishing a broadsword, rushed towards the O'Cathains.
'Nay! Nay!' shouted Angus. 'Finvola came to me in love and shall gang hame in love. I should a kept me word. I just couldnay bear to part wi' ma wee bonnie lass.'

The O'Cathains stayed overnight. It was a long sorrowful night for both families. As dawn broke, the O'Cathains made their way to the Firth, carrying the body of their beloved Finvola and, with her on board, set sail for home.

The people of the Roe Valley had waited sadly for their beloved Finvola's return. Slowly, respectfully, they followed the cortège along a narrow track to the Abbey near Doonegiven (Dungiven).

Nature donned its best for the chieftain's daughter: ferns unfurled fronds of lush green; cascades of hawthorn blossom let sweet-smelling petals fall on to mourners; purple violets perfumed the air. Golden gorse glowed under midday sun as the O'Cathains reverently laid the remains of their beloved Finvola to rest in the abbey grounds. The gem of the Roe was back where she belonged.

Copy of a page from the Book of Kells.

The Drumcete Convention

(Mullagh Hill Limavady 584 A.D.)

Dara O'Maolain was pleased with his day's work. He had been up since daybreak but did not mind at all. He loved helping Colmcille by mixing inks, transported from distant lands, for him to use on the illuminations of the Book of Kells which he had been working on since arriving on the island of Iona.

Dara had been out on the rocks for hours, gathering feathers for quills. He knew which feathers made the best quills for the different sizing of letters and elaborate Celtic designs used in his master's writings of the sacred scriptures. He enjoyed working with Colmcille. Sure hadn't he left his family and sweetheart to follow the holy and learned man all the way across the Irish Sea to Scotland?

Although Dara's body was weary, sleep did not come easily to him that particular night. His head buzzed with excitement: he had been chosen to travel back to Ulster, to his home in the valley of the River Roe, to see history in the making. King Aed, (Hugh) the high king of Ireland, from Kells, had called for a great gathering of kings, chieftains and clergy at Drumcete, high above the River Roe, to sort out two important concerns.

Firstly, there was the issue of Dal Riata, the Christian region of western Scotland which wanted total independence from Ireland. King Aed collected taxes from Dal Riata, as well as from Ireland.

The disgruntled inhabitants of Dal Riata received very little in return.

Colmcille was cousin to both kings. A prince, and a priest, he was loved and respected in both countries. Aed was putting pressure on Colmcille to oppose Aiden, the peace-loving king of Dal Riata, who wanted to improve the lives of his people.

The second problem was the position and power of the bards. The bards were very important, well-educated writers, poets, musicians and storytellers. When kings and chieftains fought battles the job of the bard was to sing the praises of the leaders and ridicule the enemy. Some bards were so powerful it was said that they could make boils, as big as stones, appear on the faces of their enemies, or anyone against whom they bore a grudge.

It was considered that there were too many bards: lots of them poked fun at the high king and chieftains, in their stories and songs, and kings do not like to be criticized. Not many people could read or write and the bards provided news and knowledge which they recited in poems and songs. Wherever bards travelled and performed throughout the country, they had to be paid and given free accommodation and food, in even the poorest of homes. That was the law. With so many of them, it had become expensive.

Dara wondered how these problems could be solved without bloodshed. When he was a boy, some of the other lads had poked fun at him for not joining in fights. They gave him the nickname

Coinin, meaning rabbit.

Dara pondered another dilemma: he was thinking of Aoife, the girlfriend he left behind, in the Roe Valley, when he followed Colmcille. He had begged her to accompany him.
'This is your dream, Dara, not mine. I must not leave my father alone,' she had protested. 'He cannot manage without me.'

Angered and hurt by Aoife's rebuff, Dara sailed to Iona without her. Now he wondered if she had found a husband while he was gone. He could hardly dare hope that she was still unmarried. None of the girls he had met in Scotland could compare to Aoife. He thought maybe he had been wrong to accompany Colmcille but the alternative would have been a life of soldiering, which abhorred him.

The sound of rain battering the roof of the monastery roused Dara from his reverie and he groaned loudly. Mighty waves crashed on the shore.

The following morning Dara examined the rowing boat that was to carry them back to Ulster: he thought it would take a miracle to get them there safely. A crew of twelve knelt on the beach while Colmcille led prayers. Suddenly the rain stopped, sun shone and, by the time they were loaded up, waves were lapping more gently against the sides of the boat.

It was a long arduous journey; the wind was against them but the crew-men were strong. God was with them. They sang psalms, chatted and told tall tales of terrible storms they had endured when waves were hundreds, maybe a thousand, feet high.

The sun was setting behind Inishowen by the time they reached Lough Foyle. Where the River Roe flowed into the Lough, they turned their boats and paddled towards the woods in which they planned to strike camp.

The smell of roasting pig, the beating of drums, and the laughter and shouts of so many men at the camp, overwhelmed Dara's senses at first: he had become used to the silence of the monastery. There was great excitement and debate among the men. Some were betting their horses, or boats, on the outcome of the convention that was due to take place at Drumcete. In a clearing, among the oak trees, there were wrestling and spear-throwing competitions. In some tents there were serious discussions but a general air of gaiety filled the valley.

Out of the gloaming, a young messenger came galloping recklessly on a large chestnut mare. He was from The Rough Fort, a couple of miles from camp – a haven of King Aed and his men.

Dara was suspicious when the lad asked him to accompany him to the fort; he was also curious and reckoned that he would be well able to defend himself against the youth, if need be.

Before long, Dara was climbing steep-sided earthworks. When he heard women's chatter and laughter he wondered if they were playing some kind of joke, to humiliate him but, as he drew closer,

Dara could hardly believe his eyes. Stooping over the fire, in the glow of the dying sun, was Aoife, looking even more beautiful than when he had last seen her.

They had little time to talk because the women were preparing food for the king's men. They did not want to hang around in case they would have trouble with soldiers but, as Dara drank in the beauty of the lough, the sea and the mountains of Loughermore, Inishowen, Binevenagh, Keady and Benbradagh, he could feel his heart softening. He had missed the valley as much as he had missed Aoife. Being there with her was what he wanted most. He truly belonged in that special place and decided that, if necessary, he would join an army's ranks if, by doing so, he could remain there with Aoife.

Dara raced back to the camp with wings on his feet, hoping he had not been missed. As scribe, he was supposed to stay close to Colmcille at all times, recording anything of importance. Colmcille was meticulous and expected nothing less from his servants. Luckily for Dara, Colmcille was already snoring loudly in his tent.

The following morning, as Dara followed Colmcille up Mullagh Hill at Drumcete, he felt privileged to be in the company of the highest-ranking noblemen and clergy in the whole of Ireland and Dal Riata. The Coinin had come a long way since he was last there as a boy, almost afraid of his own shadow.

The smell of freshly cut grass wafted over the gathered crowd of noblemen. Some of the leaders wore heavy gold jewellery that had been in their families for centuries; their torcs were richly decorated with elaborate Celtic designs; they wore thick chains around their necks to show people they were rich and powerful. Colmcille wore a simple woollen gown.

In Sligo, a few years previously, Colmcille had copied sacred documents belonging to Finian, his teacher. Finian insisted on having the copies but, because he had put so much time and effort into them, Colmcille refused. A bloody battle ensued and hundreds of good men were killed.

Afterwards the high king made a declaration: ‘To every cow its calf; to every book its copy.’ This was the first copyright law: the documents belonged to Finian. Colmcille had to return the copies to their rightful owner.

After the law was passed, Colmcille realised he had been in the wrong. Too much blood had been spilt because of him. To make reparation to God, Colmcille promised to leave Ireland and convert as many people to Christianity as had been killed in the battle. He declared that he would never set foot on Irish soil again. To avoid breaking his promise, he returned as a peacemaker with sods of earth from Iona tied to his feet.

A lot of discussion at the convention went over Dara’s head: he was imagining his future with Aoife. Occasionally his daydream was interrupted by the high king’s loud and angry words. Dara understood Aed's proud nature and love of riches but also knew he could be fair and honest.

Colmcille spent many hours facilitating negotiations between the two men, bargaining with them and placating them when tempers became frayed. King Aiden believed it was wrong for the High King of Ireland to collect taxes from the people of Dal Riata. His people had become angry; they wanted their taxes paid to him so that he could build good houses, roads and schools.

Before the sun set over the Foyle, the two sides reached agreement: Dal Riata was to be given independence from Ireland, providing the people would promise to come to Ireland's aid if necessary. Colmcille fasted in thanksgiving to God for the good outcome.

The next few days' discussions were devoted to trying to solve the problem of the bards. The High King wanted to ban them completely. He did not take criticism well and some were merciless in their insolent rants against him. Again Colmcille, by talking and listening to all sides involved, managed to secure agreement. A middle course was adopted: bards' numbers were to be cut and strict rules laid down regarding their behaviour. The bards' new role would be to teach, collect stories and spread information. They were to be paid for their work and would not have to rely on people's generosity. Bards performed an important role in Irish culture for another thousand years. It is because of them that we know so much about life in Celtic Ireland.

The Drumcete gathering partied all through the night. They danced Highland flings and Irish jigs to the lively music of bagpipes, fiddles and harps. While they waited for boar to roast on a great spit, they dined on salmon and trout from the River Roe, and wild mushrooms which women had gathered at dawn. Pigeons, stuffed with wild garlic, were served with sorrel and watercress. Wild strawberries, sweetest at that time of year, were served with cream which was thick and plentiful. Men drank locally-brewed beer and whiskey. The celebration was long remembered.

Dara could not enjoy himself fully because he was nervous about telling Colmcille his plans to remain in Ireland. Colmcille had been good to him and had taught him many skills, as well as reading and writing. The previous year he had sent him to a master to learn the art of illuminated writing. The work had excited Dara and the master had told him he had a great gift. Dara knew that such gifts from God were not to be wasted but celebrated and shared. His heart ached for Aoife however, and he knew that she would not want to live separated from her father, or her beloved Roe Valley.

The next day the kings, chieftains, priests and scribes all joined with the monks of nearby Tamlaght Finlagan monastery, overlooking Lough Foyle, to fast, pray and give thanks to God for such a successful, peaceful convention.

'Colmcille tells me you might be looking for a job with us, Dara,' smiled an old stooped monk.

'I suppose so,' mumbled Dara. Could Colmcille read minds?

‘I do have eyes in my head!’ Colmcille laughed at the surprised look on Dara’s face. ‘The superior’s hands aren’t what they used to be, so he needs someone to help him with his illuminated writings. I’ve told him that there’s no better man for the job than yourself. There’s a wee house there for you and that dark-haired beauty, should you wish to get wed.’

Later, at Magilligan Point, Aoife and Dara sat astride a big chestnut stallion and waved goodbye as the boats of King Aiden and Colmcille sailed out the mouth of Lough Foyle and onwards towards Dal Riata.

‘Ah, Dara, if we live to be a hundred years old we’ll never see the likes of this again. These days will be spoken about for centuries to come’, sighed Aoife.

Dara nodded. He remained silent for a long time, thinking about how privileged he was to have been part of such a momentous occasion in Irish history.

A few weeks later, Aoife and Dara were married at the monastery in Tamlaght Finlagan. They lived long and happy lives together. Their children had children and their descendants are as many as the leaves on a hazel tree.

At that very special time Ireland was known all over Europe as the land of saints and scholars.

Binevenagh

(Viewed from Mullagh Hill)

By Iris Forrest

You can see me best in all my glory
during the summer days,
when the light of rainbow colours
fill the canvas of your eyes.

I suggest you climb to summits
parallel to mine and
once there, stop and stare with narrowed eyes
at my magnificence, at the edge of your valley.

I give out strength in exchange for awe.
You wonder at my presence, my endurance
whilst the clock of life ticks in your heart,
I know that I will see tomorrow's dawn.

A Scottish bagpipe player.

The Piper McQuillan

The cold damp Halloween weather played havoc with Robbie's arthritis, keeping him indoors. Perched on the garden wall, staring straight at him, was a strange bird with hooded eyes and hooked beak. Robbie rapped the window with his stick - the bird did not budge. A dark shadow moved towards the front door. The bird remained still.

The old man hobbled to answer loud knocking. Bad news, he thought, or maybe just tricksters. At the door stood a short angular man with straggly pitch-black hair, sharp nose, sharp eyes and sharp chin. He looked the old man up and down before extending a bony hand.

'Robbie Hamilton? My name is Nick MacQuillan.'

Robbie hesitated, just a moment, before shaking a hand that was limp and ice-cold. Bruce, Robbie's old collie, whined then slunk into the cold night, tail between his legs.

'I'm researching a musician known as The Piper MacQuillan; he lived in, or around, the Drumsurn area in the middle of the seventeenth century. They told me at the pub that you are a storyteller, one with all the old tales.'

'Are you a historian?'

'No, I'm a piper.'

'Did you say your name is MacQuillan? Any relation?'

'Maybe.'

'Well, you'd better come in and we can talk in the heat. If I'm not mistaken, those are snow-clouds.'

The dark stranger sidled past Robbie and sat on a chair in a shadowy corner of the room. Robbie did not believe in switching on the lamp too early: he liked to tell stories by the light of the fire.

'Well now,' said Robbie, 'there were MacQuillans living at Dunluce Castle. Some of them were musicians but, as far as I know, there was only one Piper MacQuillan around these parts. I'll tell you what I know. Mind you, you might not like it for it's a strange story. To be honest, there might not be one word of truth in it.'

'Go on.'

'A wee drop of hot whiskey before we start? It's medicinal, you know. Helps keep out the cold.'

Fire whispered in the grate. Robbie was beginning to enjoy himself; there was nothing he liked better than telling stories to shorten the evening. He padded into the kitchen to prepare the drinks.

'Do you play the pipes, Mr. Hamilton?'

'Robbie. Just call me Robbie. Naw. Not any more. I have had a bad chest for years. It's this oul' house: the damp gets into your lungs as well as your joints.'

'Would you mind if I gave them a blast?'

'Not at all. 'I'm sure they're not in great shape, like myself,' laughed Robbie. The smells of sugar, cloves and whiskey enveloped him in a warm glow. He could hear the old bagpipes wheezing and rasping in the other room. It was a sound that stirred memories of pipe-competitions he had attended many years before.

Suddenly the cottage became alive - Robbie had never heard playing like it. 'You have the gift, son. You really do. You could well be a descendant of your man. Now, here's the story of

MacQuillan the piper as I heard it passed down, you understand, from generation to generation.

'Not long after the Ulster Plantation, when our ancestors came here from Scotland and England, there was a piper by the name of MacQuillan: a strange sort of chap, nobody liked him. He rented a wee house by Legavannon Pot, from a man named McCloskey. Now when I say rented that's not strictly true for, as far as I know, he never paid a penny in rent and McCloskey was too afraid of him to ask for money.

'MacQuillan, like yourself, was a great piper – the best anyone had ever heard. He played such soulful music it touched the hearts of all who heard it, bringing tears to their eyes. Then, when he'd play a happy tune, everyone would be up dancing and singing - even the old and the sick: their pains seemed to vanish! He also liked to play battle-music. Within minutes the whole room would be in ructions with people lashing out at each other and fists flying in all directions. Nobody knew who his people were. The Dunluce MacQuillans were gentry and they wouldn't let him anywhere near their castle at all.

'One day the priest called upon him, in the hope of saving his soul by getting him to Confession. He went so far as to offer him money to play a few hymns at Mass. Well, I believe that the answer he got from the piper was such that no decent man could repeat. MacQuillan held no truck with religion: at the mention of God he'd fly into a terrible rage.
He played his music in the dark woods, for birds and animals. Some of the locals thought he was one of the faery folk that lived in the woods around Gelvin.'

Outside, Bruce began to howl and scratch at the back door.
'Will you excuse me for one minute, 'til I see what's wrong with that wee dog of mine.'

When Robbie opened the door, the dog skulked away into the bushes. 'I do believe it's the strange bird that's been hovering about all day that has him so spooked,' Robbie explained, pouring himself another large whiskey. Nick MacQuillan had barely touched his.

'Now, I suppose I should tell you what The Piper looked like. He was a dark, thin wee man, all bony elbows and knees; as dour and contrary a fella as you're ever likely to meet. There was a meanness about him that frightened people around Drumsurn. Even the dogs in the street were afraid of him.

'Wherever he played, crowds gathered to listen, to marvel at his amazing skill. Often as not, he played vulgar tunes, the likes of which couldn't be heard in decent company.'

Robbie stopped and wondered at the stranger's sullen silence: he sat there, still as the grave, hardly touching his drink. 'Are you sure you want to hear all this?' Robbie inquired.
Nick MacQuillan nodded.

'Now, at this time, there was a lot of rebel activity in the area. Landowners feared being burned in their beds at night. Lady Cook, a widow, had a big house somewhere around Glenullin. She was of planter stock, like myself. That was enough to make her a target for the rebels.

'One night, around Christmastime in 1641, I believe it was, rebels surrounded her house. Luckily the McCloskeys had got wind of it and had sent to Coleraine for help from the army.

'When Captain Beresford and his soldiers arrived, the rebels vanished into the mountains.

'Lady Cook was not one to forget a favour too readily. Every Christmas she organised a party for all those kind people who had come to her aid. I believe the tables were laden with food. There were roasts – goose, pork and beef; pigeons stuffed and cooked in red wine; all kinds of novelties: dates, almonds, honey-cakes and spiced biscuits. There were barrels of beer and lashings of whiskey. The women were served sweet sherry in dainty glasses, no bigger than egg-cups. My mouth is watering at the thought of that big spread. The locals would have been happy enough with a lot less. But that was the way of the gentry: they never did anything by half measures.

'This particular Christmas the band of musicians, that was supposed to perform, had all contracted scarlet fever. Lady Cook asked her servants to find a musician, for it wouldn't be much of a party without music. The Piper MacQuillan was hired to play. He strutted into the room with bagpipes thrown over his shoulder. As you can imagine, more than a few eyebrows were raised at Lady Cook's choice of piper.

' "Well, Lady Cook, what tunes do you want me to play?" asked MacQuillan.

"Christmas carols. My favourite is The Coventry Carol. Can you play that one first?"

"Naw. Never heard of it."

"Well then, can you play God Before Us Into Battle? Every piper in the country knows that one."

"Naw. Not me. Never heard of it."

'Lady Cook mentioned a few better known Christmas carols. The Piper MacQuillan shook his head at every one, answering, "Naw. Never heard of it."

'Lady Cook was becoming angry: the man had no manners at all.

"Well, what can you play?"

"I can play drinking songs," he smirked.

"Play what you like then but tone them down. Remember, there are ladies present."

'The Piper MacQuillan began to play. At first some at the gathering were shocked at the kind of tunes he was playing but he played so beautifully they were soon up dancing. Those who could not dance tapped their feet and swayed to the music.

'Just before food was served the minister rose to say grace. At the sight of the clergyman, the piper's face darkened. He strode out through the doors, leaving his pipes behind. People bent their heads and joined the minister, thanking God for the food they were about to eat. As soon as they had finished Piper MacQuillan returned to the hall and ate a hearty meal.

"I'm surprised that you hired that man. You know, I truly believe that he is the devil incarnate," the minister whispered to Lady Cook.

"He is certainly crude and arrogant but you should hear him play."

'After the meal was over, and the guests had eaten their fill, the Piper played The Desperate Battle. Rage seemed to take hold of every man and woman in the room: they were fighting, throwing punches, smashing dishes. There wasn't a man in the hall who didn't get a black eye or a bloody nose that night.

'The women were nearly as bad: pulling hair, scratching, biting - screaming abuse. Lady Cook could hardly believe her eyes - these people had stood in prayer only minutes before!

'She ordered the Piper to stop playing. He ignored her and continued to the end of the tune.

"Does the Lady not know that it is an insult to interrupt a musician? I'm off – I'll never set foot in this place again!" he shouted.

'Well, I'm sure you can imagine that Lady Cook had never been spoken to in such a manner before. She was speechless. The Piper stormed off, cursing and swearing. Lady Cook called a servant to see him off her property.

'The whole countryside had a ghostly look; the moon cast pale cold light as the servant followed the Piper outside into the snow. MacQuillan stormed through the gate, roaring and shouting, and disappeared in the direction of Drumbane Fort, leaving tracks in the freshly fallen snow.

'There was something strange about the tracks. The servant got down on his knees to have a better look. What he saw chilled him to the bone: these were no human footprints. The prints were those of a cloven hoof - the mark of a beast!

'Now the poor man nearly had a heart attack on the spot. By the time he managed to stagger inside he was as pale as a ghost. Lady Cook had to revive him with a large glass of brandy. The minister sat praying with him all night, in an attempt to calm his nerves.

'Well, the Piper MacQuillan was never seen after that night. Some locals thought he really was the devil and that he had returned to hell. Others said he got trapped inside a cave in the mountains around Drumsurn and that the sighing of his trapped spirit can still be heard to this very day.

'If you want my opinion, I believe he just moved away, as pipers did in those days. Maybe he took the boat to Scotland. That, my friend, is the story of The Piper MacQuillan. Make of it what you will.'

Robbie took another sip from his glass. Storytelling always gave him a thirst. The stranger sat still in the flickering shadows. His whiskey glass, almost full, remained on the coffee table.

'Well, Nick, what did you make of the story?'

A thin smile spread across Nick MacQuillan's face.

'I'm glad that The Piper MacQuillan is still remembered after all this time. It's a pity that the old tunes he played are mostly forgotten now. It's late, so I'll be making tracks. Good night, Robbie, and thank you for your hospitality.'

Normally Robbie felt warmed by a visitor's presence but, when he shook hands with Nick MacQuillan, he shivered. Maybe it was the cold night: it was unusual to get snow at Halloween, but the ground was covered in a thick white blanket.

'Why don't I call you a taxi? It's no weather to be out walking.'

'No. It's a real treat for me to be in the cold. Anyway I haven't far to go. I'll enjoy the walk.'

Robbie leant against the doorjamb watching Nick MacQuillan

disappear in the moonlight. Suddenly a shiver shook his whole body. He was overcome, his strength seeping away. Then he laughed - whiskey was playing tricks on his mind.
He whistled; Bruce came bounding towards him, almost knocking him down. 'You didn't like him either, eh boy?'

Inside, with the lights on, Robbie began to feel foolish. It was the night that was in it, the whiskey and the story he had told, that was making him feel so strange. He picked up the drink he had given to Nick MacQuillan, opened the door and flung the glass at the garden wall, smashing it in a thousand pieces. The strange bird flew off into the night.

Robbie locked and bolted the doors, failing to notice cloven footprints in melting snow.

Shane Crossagh O'Mullan

(Mid seventeenth century)

In Faughanvale on a February morning in the year of 1651, a group of young men were holding a leaping-competition, to keep themselves warm, as the cutting north wind blew in across Lough Foyle.

'How about a jump across the Faughan River?' suggested one. 'The prize is a load of shells from the shore at Ballykelly - provided by the losers of course!'

'No bother at all!' boasted good-looking Shane Crossagh O'Mullan. 'The shells will come in right and handy to fertilise the turnip field.'

Shane took three steps back and easily cleared the Faughan. Not to be outdone, the others followed but ended up in the icy river. Shane shook with laughter.

'How come you w-w-win every t-t-time?' asked his dripping friend.

'Ah did you never hear about my great-great-granda who found my great-granda, as an infant, on the side of a hill near Banagher with hares leaping over him. He had no weans of his own, so he took the baby home as a present for his wife. I reckon I must have hare-blood in my veins!'

There were, and still are, hundreds of O'Mullans (now known as Mullan) living around the valley of the Roe. In order to tell families apart, they had nicknames. Shane's family was known as the Crossagh (pockmarked) O'Mullans: one of his forefathers had smallpox and bore the scars upon his face.

Shane's stomach rumbled; his mouth watered as he thought of the rabbit stew his mother was preparing. When he reached the farm a terrible sight met his eyes: a huge battering-ram - a tree trunk suspended from a frame, was knocking his house down! The door was smashed, their bits of furniture strewn across the street. A land agent, protected by an armed guard, had served an eviction notice on Shane's family for non-payment of their ever-increasing rent. His father stood dumbstruck; his mother wept.

Shane lifted a stone and flung it at the agent, frightening the horse and making it rear.

'Any more of that behaviour and I'll have you in jail!' a soldier barked. The agent steadied his horse, laughed and galloped away, leaving an armed guard to oversee the destruction of the Crossagh O'Mullan family home.

'What's to become of us now?' his mother sobbed.

Shane sprang into action. 'Come on, Da, hitch up the donkey and cart. Ma, pull yourself together. Gather up what you can. We need our things. Sure we will just be classed as tramps, if we don't have our own belongings. There's nothing here for us now.'

The family cut a sorry but all too familiar sight, their possessions heaped upon the cart, as they headed up through Slaughtmanus and on towards the hills above Claudy. They made shelters out of bushes and slept in the woods alongside other evicted families, sharing what little they had.

Eventually Shane and his family settled in the townland of Lingwood. The soil was poor: they could barely grow enough to keep body and soul together. At night Shane dreamt he was back on the farm in Faughanvale, his feet sinking into the soft fertile soil, lining up the plough with Slieve Sneacht that sparkled in the distance on the far side of Lough Foyle.

Great anger surged through these displaced people: young men met at night to form a rebel army. They had been evicted from their farms in order to make way for the Plantation of Ulster: it was unlawful for the new Scottish and English settlers to have native Irish tenants.

Shane became the leader of a band of rapparees. On dark lonely mountain roads around Carntogher, Shane and his men practised their skills and became a disciplined group of highwaymen.

One night Shane lay in wait for a rich landowner returning from the market with gold sovereigns stuffed in his saddlebags. Shane was in high spirits. He fired a shot as the man's horse drew near, causing it to rear.

'Do as I say and you won't get hurt!' Shane warned. 'Hand over your money!'

The landowner, fearful for his life, put up no struggle: he had heard terrifying stories about cut-throat rebels.

'Now I want your coat and boots! It gets cold here on the

mountains without proper attire!'
The petrified man handed them over and Shane's men bound him hand and foot.

'Now you'll know what it's like to be cold and hungry. I bid you good night, sir. Thank you for your contribution to our cause - we are most grateful!' Shane laughed.

The rapparees galloped to their hide-out in the woods where they counted their takings and decided which poor families were in most need of money and clothing.

One bright May morning Shane stood entranced, watching birds busily building nests and bluebells casting shadows over the woodland floor. He was so captivated that he did not hear two redcoats approaching. Suddenly he felt a gun in his back.

'You are our prize for the day!' crowed one. 'We'll get extra rations for a leader like you!'
'Ah, I'm having the luck of the devil himself today!' Shane complained. 'I was on my way to pick up a bottle of the best poitin that was ever made. Now, not only do I not get a drink but I find myself on my way to jail! I don't suppose either of you gentlemen would be interested in doing a deal with me: the finest bottle of poitin for my freedom!'

The soldiers looked at each other. It was a chilly enough morning and a drop of poitin would certainly warm them up. They agreed.

'Follow me!' commanded Shane.
All three entered the woods. The soldiers were alert.
'No funny stuff, Crossagh, you hear?'
'I'm not a fool. It's just over there in a whin bush.'
Shane reached into the bush; the soldiers kept watch for Shane's men. Suddenly Shane pulled out a pike, disarmed the soldiers, and disappeared into the thicket.

Shane Crossagh and his men kept up these exploits for many years - robbing the rich to help the poor. They particularly enjoyed making their victims look ridiculous.

One late summer's evening, Shane was out shooting rabbits when he heard the clip-clop of a horse's hooves. Never one to let an opportunity pass, he leapt on to the road. The horse reared, throwing its rider. Shane pointed his gun at the fallen motionless soldier. Blood from his head darkened the road. The man was dead.

Shane stood still before removing his hat and saying a silent prayer for the man he had killed. Then, reaching down, he removed the soldier's blood-spattered gun and wiped it on the grass. He stripped the dead man of his uniform and dragged the body into the undergrowth. Shane knew that he and his two grown sons, Paudeen and Rory, would have to be very careful. Now that he had killed a soldier, the mountains would be swarming with cavalry when they discovered him missing.

On his way home, Shane called into a cottage to share some dead rabbits.

'Ah, Shane, you're a sight for sore eyes on this night,' beamed the grey-haired widow. 'All I can offer you is a cup of black tay in return for the rabbits. They'll make a lovely stew.'

'Is the cow in calf?'

'I wish to God it were so,' sighed the old woman. 'I couldn't pay my dues to the church, so the minister came this very day and took possession of my cow. Now I have no milk, butter or cheese. God only knows how I'm going to manage.'

Shane's face darkened. 'I'll do what I can. Meanwhile, here's a few sovereigns to keep you going for a while.'

The woman gave Shane a bed for the night. He was up before dawn, made his way to the minister's house, broke in and stole thirty pounds. Shane returned the cow and the money to the old lady before she was awake. Then he ran home whistling, leaping over burns and ditches, not giving the dead soldier another thought.

Within a few days Shane was captured. The soldiers were jubilant at having arrested an infamous rapparee who had evaded them for decades. They strapped irons and chains to his legs and, although he could not escape, Shane entertained the soldiers with tall tales and jokes.

The group stopped to rest on the top of Carntogher, on their way to the jail in Londonderry. The prisoner impressed the soldiers with his boasts of being able to leap further than any man alive.

He tried to persuade them to remove the manacles so that he could demonstrate his amazing agility.

'I'll give you my word that I won't try to escape. Sure, I'm alone among a dozen armed soldiers: I'm not completely crazy!' The soldiers were intrigued. They had heard stories about Shane's leaping ability and wanted to see it with their own eyes. They removed the leg-irons.

Shane made two enormous leaps. 'Well, what do you think? Is there any one of you can match me?'
As the soldiers looked around, shaking their heads at each other, Shane disappeared down the mountain like a hare. He raced all the way to Limavady.

Soldiers ran hot on his heels, seeking directions when they lost sight of him. Eyewitnesses were unreliable: 'I saw him head for Magilligan'.
'I saw him heading for Coleraine.'
'No, he went towards Ballykelly.'

Shane was having a bit of a breather behind huge grey stones (ancient pagan standing stones) in a field in Magheramore belonging to another O'Mullan, a kinsman of his own. Peeping from behind the tallest stone, he could see soldiers approach the Knockenduns. He had to get going or they would soon catch him.

He headed over Barnault, towards the Ness Woods, for cover.

Close behind, he could hear dogs barking, hooves clopping, men shouting. Reaching cliffs above the Burntollet River, he looked down into the chasm: if he were to fall, he'd surely die. If he stopped - it would be the gallows for him.

Shane took a deep breath and ran towards the swollen river, throwing all his weight towards the other side. Miraculously he made it safe and sound on to solid ground. He laughed over at the soldiers.

'You'll never catch Shane Crossagh O'Mullan!' he shouted above the noise of the swirling river.

'Bravo, brave Shane Crossagh!' shouted an old man out walking with his dog. Shane waved and grinned before disappearing.

Not all planters were enemies of Shane Crossagh O'Mullan. Some of them were decent men, good landlords prepared to break the law and rent property to the native Irish. They did not exploit the people.

One such planter was Henry Carey who lived in Dungiven Castle. Shane had saved Henry's life once, when he was attacked by another group of rapparees. 'Save your fury for the heartless land-agents and their masters!' Shane admonished them. 'Carey is a decent man!'

One summer's afternoon as Shane and his comrades were drinking in a secret room in Fowler's public house, outside Dungiven, General Napier and a small band of redcoats entered the building. The owner was a planter, a friend of Shane's; he let Shane use a room with peep-holes and listening-posts so that he could see and hear wealthy travellers' talk, and he received a portion of the spoils.

The landlord teased the general about his inability to catch the notorious Shane Crossagh and his sons. General Napier gave a thunderous roar, 'That little upstart Irish thief is no match for an English officer! I shall track him down and he shall hang like a dog before this week is through!'

'Better men than you have failed,' an ancient man laughed quietly into his pint of stout. Shane knew that Napier's men were transporting gold, to pay the army in Londonderry. The barman continued pressing alcohol on Napier's men until darkness began to fall, giving Shane and his sons time to set up an ambush at a narrow bridge in Feeny.

The Crossagh O'Mullan's drove ash sticks into sods which they had built up on either side of the bridge; in the growing darkness they looked like dozens of guns.

As General Napier approached the bridge Shane shot his horse, causing mayhem. Paudeen and Rory fired volleys around the startled soldiers.

'Surrender to Shane Crossagh or not a single man will be spared!' Shane ordered.

The general and his men surrendered. They were taken prisoner by the Crossagh O'Mullans who swapped clothes with them, before tying their hands behind their backs. Weapons and horses were taken as trophies.

'Now I'll have your uniform, Napier. I do believe the colours would suit me much better than they do you!' Shane mocked. Silently, the General obeyed. The humiliation of having to wear the rough clothes of a rapparee was almost too much for him to bear.

Dressed as redcoats, they marched Napier and his men twelve miles before putting them on the Foyle ferry which would return them to the English camp, in the walled city of Londonderry. Shane and his sons then galloped away to their hide-out in the Sperrins, wearing English army uniforms, their pockets filled with gold.

However, the jubilation of the daredevil rapparees did not last long. Napier quadrupled the number of spies and promised even more money for the Crossagh O'Mullans' capture. The reward was too much of a temptation for one poor Dungiven weaver: he gave information which led to them being captured and sentenced to death by hanging.

Henry Carey was influential enough to grant Shane a pardon, on condition that he give up all illegal activities.
Shane was worried about his sons' fate: "I need pardons for Rory and Paudeen too.'

'I can only pardon one prisoner each year,' Carey explained..

'Then hang me too – I cannot live without my sons!'

As Shane, Rory and Paudeen walked out on to the gallows, hand in hand, the crowd cheered loudly. The Crossagh O'Mullans held their heads high; not a sign of fear crossed their faces as they awaited death.

They were hanged at the Diamond in Londonderry in 1772. Their bodies are buried in an unmarked grave at Banagher Old Church, high in the Sperrins.

Notes

- Nowadays the mountain road between Dungiven and Maghera is called The Glenshane Pass after the highwayman, Shane Crossagh O'Mullan.
- On Carntogher three cairns mark the spot where Shane made his leaps. In years gone by it was a place where people made visits on Palm Sunday.
- In the Ness Woods, above the Burntollet River, is a spot which is known as Shane's Leap.
- The General's Bridge in Feeny is called after General Napier.

Glenshane

By Grainne Shaw

Patch-worked splendour
Surrounds.

Swirling dark blue mist and rain
Rest upon your weary shoulders.

Lonely, desolate, wilderness
Yet almost touching civilisation.

Biting wind, sometimes blinding sun,
Clear, fresh and clean

Gateway to work, to family, to recreation,
to something else.

Glenshane means I'm almost home;
Glenshane Pass.